The Rise of
NETHANEL

Andrew R. Bennett

The Rise of Nethanel

by Andrew R. Bennett

Photo Credits:

Front Cover photo and interior image from 123RF.com
Back cover photo by Geraldine Jerome

Copyright ©2020 by Andrew R. Bennett

ISBN 979-8671930917

Printed in the United States of America

PRGott Books Publishing Service
Norway, Maine
www.prgottbooks.net

For my Mother

–CHAPTER 1–

Rail had to be extremely careful going up the last twenty yards. It had been raining the past two days and the steep, moss covered ledge in front of him was dangerously slick. The skid trail he was following was more a cliff then a road. The gouge marks in the rock bore mute testimony to the desperate state of the logger who had slid down through here the last time the wood had been cut.

These gouge marks would help Rail. He determined that if he kept low and took his time, then he would probably make it to the crest of the hill in front of him. Just beyond this narrow crest was what he had been looking for. There was a shallow gully up there before the mountain jumped up even steeper to a last shaggy face that guarded the real summit.

On that face, held in place by the sheer will power of two hundred year old roots which drove down into the cracking ledge before sweeping up around the huge boulders which had stood with the trees in an uneasy alliance to remain in place against the bosom of that unkind hill; there were the huge oak trees which the loggers had not wanted to get for any reason.

Besides being on very rough, difficult ground, the trees here, by and large, were generally of little commercial value. Though tall and of impressive girth, many of these trees were either obviously hollow or promising to be so. A majority of them had large, open seams which ran for considerable distances up their tortured trunks. Only once in a while could a younger, relatively decent specimen be seen tucked away up where eagles and ravens liked to safely rest before they headed down below to where they might succeed in finding food, if they persisted in searching long enough. This was a northern desert where the oak and beech trees passed themselves off as boreal cactus. But the trees here were big and unbothered and what Rail needed.

This was the time of the year to find the Hen of the Woods. Just one of these mushrooms, growing around the base of an ancient oak, could weigh over a hundred pounds. They grew in great, leafy masses which were more like a thick, rugged lettuce then a solitary, ordinary mushroom. Their price had been going up in recent years. They were almost at the point of being scarce. The forest down below wasn't what it used to be.

After suffering for several long decades, the forestry industry in New England had bounced back for a while. Due to arrangements made during the latter part of the twentieth century, the masses of Asia had risen to a middle-class status. Then they built factories, armies, bridges and houses—lots of wood houses, complete with wooden furniture

For a long time, the wood for this building boom came from rain forests. Then one day someone in New York or Brussels got their shoes wet walking near a waterfront somewhere, and a correctness machine got directly into high gear. Soon there were actual sanctions, and before long the flood of wood from the tropics became a trickle. But the demand for wood didn't slow down in the least.

Maine had always maintained a "sustainable forestry practice"—in theory anyway. Of course, these practices tended to be unbelievably elastic in nature depending on who knew whom. Demand grew and grew until every conceivable tree was drooled over and finally, with very few tears, cut. Even the old oak trees where Rail used to find his Hen of the Woods were eagerly smashed to the ground and sent into the maw of the Asian housing boom. There was only one place left to go—up.

Up here, he figured, there would still grow the fluffy hens. He had almost given up the practice because they had become so difficult to locate, but then the prices began to rise. The same Asian masses who devoured the wood and the Maine lobsters, soon discovered the hens. Rail had always considered his mushroom hunting a hobby, but now it was a hobby that all his other hobbies revolved around.

When he went golfing, he often would end up spending as much time figuring out how he could sneak onto some land to check out big trees in the fall as he did lining up his putts. The rich homes around the golf courses always presented a challenge, but if Rail figured a hen was in the offering, then risks would have to be taken. If the land wasn't obviously posted and if there were no vicious dogs about, then a discreet, early morning visit just might prove to be a cure for some pressing financial problem which was currently vexing him.

He loved to fish, especially in brooks and rivers. The woods around these bodies of water were supposed to be protected by law, but as the valuable big trees grew scarcer, then the waters grew warmer and warmer as more and more shade was removed. Wood was cut whether it was legal or not. Most of the hens growing there clucked and were gone. Not all, but the ones that remained were guarded with justifiable jealousy.

Like a lot of Americans, Rail found that the more the politicians touted the economy and the remaining benefits of agreements like NAFTA, the more these worthy citizens would crow and preen, the poorer he got. The costs of living went up, while his wages mostly remained the same. Or, if his wages did, by some accident, go up, his hours would go down. He didn't push it any, though. At least he had a job. After all, if those folks over there in Asia were going to go up, then somebody would just have to come down. And, if it were true that globalization meant less time on the job, then it was also true that he had more free time to do the things that mattered almost as much, like hunting.

Any kind of hunting was good, and, as time went on, that activity became a lot more than a recreational pursuit. All his life he had driven around this region, looking up and wondering what the bear went over the mountain to see. Now, with the price of the mushrooms doubling every year, he figured that it was time to get a bear's eye view of the roughest, most remote mountaintops he could. He stopped bird and deer hunting around his traditional spots and headed up to the forgotten places up in the far mountains. Especially if he could make out some ancient hardwood stands on those forbidding slopes.

The area where Rail now stood was a place he had targeted the fall before when he was deer hunting. His hunting buddies had lamented his absence from their hunts, but Rail was glad he had persevered and had located this stand. It was impossible for him to believe that a gargantuan hen wasn't up there pecking away at the base of some rotten behemoth of an oak. He surveyed the hill above him for some means of ascending it. This wasn't going to be an easy, nor even safe, climb.

The mushrooms he sought were big and bulky, so he carried on his back a large wicker basket that his grandfather had made from some brown ash, which had been growing on the edge of a swamp that came up beside a front pasture. It was old but still in superb shape. Originally, it had been used for trapping, then for ice fishing and now for bringing home the Hen of the Woods, hopefully anyway. Right now, all it had in there were Rail's sandwiches and a jug of water.

Rail slipped off a strap and took the basket off. The dinner and water would stay here on the ledge while he went above with the empty basket. When he got hungry enough or thirsty enough to come back down, then it would be time to go home. Hopefully, that would be before dark. Folks didn't like it when he didn't get home before dark. He wasn't too fond of it himself.

This year if he found enough hens, he decided that he would purchase a new phone. As he took his lunch out of the basket, he could feel his large hunting knife dangling from his belt. He knew that in this sort of terrain he should have a cell phone dangling there instead. He had smashed the last one he owned in a nasty fall. He hated the thought of another one bothering him all day long, but nevertheless he knew that he should have one just the same.

That being decided he got the basket balanced and took a typically long step toward the hill. The slope in front of him would have been a challenge for most people but not for

Rail. Though undeniably skinny to an inordinate degree, the real attribute which contributed to his nickname was that, despite his slenderness, he was, as his uncle had muttered to a friend one day, "... tough as a rail, too."

Quietly sitting in the shade, his uncle had been observing his nephew's unrelenting restlessness and unyielding energy out in a stifling hay field beyond. He marveled at Rail's remorselessness and wondered if that life force would be contained in a constructive manner. No, not everyone was cut out to hunt for the Hen of the Woods, but Rail was.

Rail now checked the sky. It had been raining a tropical sort of rain the past few days. It was very humid, and Rail knew that rain sometimes bred rain. Looking up beyond the steep slope in front of him, he could see that this was probably one of those times. The clouds beyond the mountain were sullen and growing into each other. It was time to get cracking.

With an eye borne of experience, he quickly decided on a path that he figured would probably work. The remnants of some old deer tracks verified his choice. In difficult terrain, the deer always seemed to know where to go. The climb wasn't as bad as he had feared even if clumps of forest ferns forced him to go slower then he would have liked, what with the dark clouds frowning on the near horizon. Still, though the slope was sharp enough to necessitate using his hands almost as much as his legs, his long stringy legs kept him solidly anchored as he advanced up the hill at a reasonable pace.

However, the higher up he went, the presence of the ferns became more of a nuisance then he had initially anticipated. Besides covering up loose rocks or rotten wood that perpetually threatened to make his climb difficult or even downright dangerous, the ferns also tended to congregate around the base of the trees, making it difficult to tell whether or not there were any mushrooms hiding there.

It was not uncommon to hike many miles and spend many days chasing geese instead of collecting hens. That is why they commanded the price they did. It was always a sobering experience to come to the realization that a great location, a sure thing, was, in fact, a complete bust.

Most people couldn't handle it. After several exhausting, futile years, they would come to the conclusion that life was too short and apt to be a lot shorter if they kept killing themselves searching for what was obviously not there. They never developed their mushroom eyes. They didn't have what it took. They would go through something like what Rail was now experiencing and quit. They would hang up their baskets and head for the nearest couch.

Now Rail, he might have a sober moment or two, but he never got depressed. That same irrepressible energy and inner strength that his uncle had marveled at would come boiling up and carry him over the next river, the next mountain, or whatever got between him and his objectives.

Up ahead of him the slope which Rail was now perched on grew even steeper. But it wasn't a cliff. It could be done, and Rail made up his mind that he was going to do it. If he could get through the current section that he was on, it looked to him that the hill just might moderate up toward the top. There were big trees up there which needed to be checked out.

He hadn't climbed a hundred yards before, sure enough, he glanced to his left and spied the telltale shape and color of a hen growing around the base of a surprisingly small tree. There were rocks and ferns in the way, but he knew that it was there. An old dead oak effectively provided a bridge for him to more-or-less crawl along, and after a few minutes he was able to make his way up to the valuable mushroom. Then, just as he was releasing his hunting knife to cut off the hen at its base, there came a low rumble of thunder emanating from somewhere near the other side mountain. He would have to hurry now.

Ordinarily, Rail would have been disappointed with the size of the hen beneath him, for the mushroom accurately reflected the size of the young tree that it was growing on. However, Rail knew the thunderstorm was nearby and that he was in a very exposed and finicky position. He slipped off his basket and went to work. He carefully knelt down beside the base of the tree.

The incline of the mountain was so great that he had to dig one foot into some rare soft ground while getting the other one wedged down in front of a large rock to keep from sliding. Once he got sufficiently anchored, he proceeded to place the basket on the ground and kept it in place with his chest, as he turned the basket's opening toward the mushroom.

Rail had to keep his mind on his feet as he pushed his knife toward the base of the leathery structure of the hen's mass. Once he got his knife positioned in the right place, then the mushroom cut easily enough, but it was about twenty inches from the point nearest him to the far end of the hen, almost to the other side of the tree. Stretching to cut it all put a lot of pressure on his feet, but experience got him through the task. It—the mushroom—wasn't anywhere near as high and full as he would have liked, but once he got it all secured in his basket, then Rail was content. He figured there was ten to fifteen pounds of Hen of the Woods there, enough to justify his efforts getting up there. And more importantly, he had discovered a new place to locate them, which was never guaranteed. He was nearly in a state of mushroom ecstasy.

That state was short-lived. A fat raindrop and a rapid diminishment of light told him that he needed to retreat off the mountain as soon as he could. Down in the valleys you could trace the development of thunderstorms and gauge accurately the amount of time you had left to get to cover. Up here, on the other hand, Rail knew that the minute you heard thunder, you were already in the storm.

Suddenly everything became immediate and not fun. The ancient tree trunk, which had provided him with a path to the hen, now threatened to break apart if he moved back across it too quickly. If that occurred, if the tree broke apart with him on it, the ground below it offered no refuge, no safe place to land. Even as this was becoming readily apparent to Rail as he crept along, even as he perceived his doom down below, the light around him failed almost completely, as a deep, nearby rumble of thunder poked playfully at him and prodded him along, while the old tree crumbled behind him.

Rail was sort of glad when he managed to get back to the place where he had originally spotted the mushroom, now in his basket. It was still a long way back down to where his dinner bag sat waiting on the ledge. A couple of gigantic raindrops found their way directly down his neck, as a wink of lightning coyly threatened to vaporize him. Without further ado, he dumped himself down the steep slope, catching at roots and rocks and random things with an amazing lack of concern that he knew he could never duplicate again in a thousand years.

He was exhausted and sweating profusely by the time he staggered up to his water jug and dinner. To his left, looking down the hill, was a clump of low hemlock and spruce. Being in open on a ledge was no place to be. Rail headed for the low trees.

Hustling along, Rail soon got away from the bald face of the open ledge and entered into a short line of young spruce, which guarded a grove of stunted, gnarled ancient hemlock that had, in their patient way, prospered beneath the protective brow of the hill behind them for well over a hundred years. Rail noticed right away, however, that one of their number had been blown apart by a lightning strike many years before. He noticed a deer trail that would lead him down deeper into the hemlock stand where he would be in less danger. He made a mental note to use this path when he came this way again.

There was a sudden hard blow, so he stopped by a huge hemlock that was growing directly beside a boulder that the ice age had dislodged from the steep hill behind him. The boulder was half the size of a house, and the hemlock had astutely used this rocky mass to keep itself upright for over two centuries. Rail could stand right under the boulder to get out of the rain, which was now coming down with good intensity. He took a drink of water and waited for the storm to slack off.

On the neighboring mountain, not all that far away, he saw a spot of sunlight break through. He decided to eat a sandwich as he waited for the storm to pass. He was chewing away contentedly on the previous night's ham when the rain suddenly let up. As is often the case in dark and gloomy places, the increased presence of light changed the perspective of his immediate surroundings tremendously.

Not too far below him was a narrow, sunken bench guarded by the same hemlock and rock rubble which now sheltered him. Beyond that bench, Rail could tell that there promised to be a grand view of the territory below. While Rail ate, he glanced around for signs of porcupine or fisher cats. Usually in places like this, with big rocks, there would be some signs of their struggles, but not here.

Not enough water maybe, Rail thought as he chewed away, wondering at the desert-like quality of this remote place.

Then the sun came out and he stopped chewing. Somehow, he had missed it before, but the sunbeam now pierced the interior beneath a scrubby spruce tree, which grew along the edge of the narrow bench below. The sunbeam had guided Rail's eye to something lying beneath the spruce. Ordinarily, Rail would have known right away what he was looking at, but in this case, the white largeness had been partially obscured by the scrubbiness of the spruce and had confused him momentarily. He threw what was left of his sandwich to the ground and headed down to the spruce.

He hadn't gone too far when he did, in fact, recognize what was lying there. Initially he didn't think too much of it. He wondered why the mice hadn't got it or, if they did, how much of it they did chew. The closer he got to it, the faster his heart rate went up.

When Rail finally did stand over it, he was astonished. The mice hadn't touched it at all, and it was worth a lot more than all the mushrooms that he would ever harvest. Before him lay the largest deer rack that he, or anyone else for that matter, would ever see. It was still attached to the skull and it was in perfect condition.

He took his basket off and, after quite a tussle, managed to get one side of the rack stuffed into it far enough to keep it in place. Rail understood the value of what he had, the undeniable magnificence of it. Now the world of humanity would know what the white-tail universe already knew—that Sejanus, lord of the upper-lower foothills of western Maine, was dead and that there was now a vacuum in that vital area which must be filled.

–CHAPTER 2–

In northern Manitoba during the early part
of the sixteenth century lived a white-tail buck
of massive proportions. Along the outermost
rim of the extreme northern white-tail range,
somewhere in the area north of Southern Indian
Lake and south of the Wolverine River, Scipio,
at a relatively early age, had decided to stake his
claim in the white-tail world.

No human ever saw him, but if they had,
they would have instantly recognized him as a
master buck of the first order. Because of the
severe climate and the presence of formidable
predators, the deer of that region were, and still
are, big. They have to be to survive the cold, the
snow, and the wolves. Then, as now, someone had
to be the biggest, and Scipio was that individual.
Maybe that's why he didn't range all that far. In
a harsh environment he felt that he had to stay
close to the places where he could most reliably

find food and water.

But even in that remote and barren world, the word got around. Scipio had star power. Over time, does would come to him from long distances. They had to have a certain disposition to do this. Although it was a distinct aberration from the norm for the does to seek out a particular buck in this manner, nevertheless it is sometimes aberrations of this kind which define success.

These does were descended from the more nomadic branches of the white-tail world. Scipio didn't travel, because somehow he knew that he was exactly where he was supposed to be. The local, typically desperate deer population got the genes they needed to thrive out at the extreme northern range. That was important, but not as important as what Scipio imparted to the wandering does who came his way.

Scipio lived his entire life in a relatively small area, but he was nevertheless an important force in the white-tail world. Whereas he was a complete homebody, some of his descendants, thanks to their mothers, turned out to be spectacular wanderers. Frequently, a generation or two would be skipped, but eventually the strength which had driven Scipio would be carried south toward the larger herds, mostly by does who would sometimes travel as much as a hundred miles before they found happiness and settled down. Bucks descended from him had tended to remain localized, but every once in a while, even one of them would break out and go on fifty-mile jaunts to spread oats that were plenty wild and plenty potent. Yes, Scipio was a huge success as a white-tail buck.

Now, northern Manitoba was a fine place for a deer of Scipio's stature, but most of his tribe had trouble recognizing that place as any sort of white-tail nirvana. Not surprisingly, therefore, the wandering gene was strongly in evidence for at least fifty years after Scipio's demise, on the female side at any rate.

A long series of favorable winters had made southern Manitoba a difficult place for a new strain of deer to get a toehold in. Generally speaking, therefore, the offspring of Scipio filtered rather rapidly down through Ontario before eventually settling down in the environs associated with the Ohio Valley. They, the dominant does, left the bucks in Ontario while continuing to infuse their daughters with the wandering gene.

All that apparently changed in the Ohio region. As a reasonably temperate area (as compared to the icy grip of Manitoba), with a lot of open edges for deer to work with, the spawn of Scipio halted their rapid advance and refurbished themselves genetically.

At first it was an invisible assimilation. It looked as though the impetus which Scipio had imparted to his lineage was about to be swallowed up by the larger whole of the Ohio Valley herd. Time went on and the assimilation into the easy living of Ohio began to close the genetic doors of Scipio's legacy. But the more doors that closed, the colder the core of that legacy became, and the better it was preserved. In the idyllic atmosphere of Ohio's apparently endless summers, the wandering gene shut down and followed everybody else round and round the unseen, unceasing eddy that it was being held in. Other traits may have waxed and waned under these conditions, but the wandering gene went into a deep state of frozen hibernation. Deeper and deeper it went, content to follow the lazy circle going nowhere.

Eventually though there were signs of change. The air around the genetic heart grew increasingly colder as the leaves of the white-tail soul fell into, and were trapped by, the eddy's endless circling. This was the power of the wandering gene. The harder that tendency—that gene—was pushed toward apparent oblivion, the stiffer and colder it became. Soon the leaves of the soul provided a bridge for the wandering gene to use. The ones that mattered, the important individuals who still carried Scipio's purpose, these few became part of a circle of ice, apart from the others and awaiting a great change, a great flood of circumstances which would thaw and move things along to another level. That change came in the early eighteenth century when the white man began to farm in earnest along the east coast.

As quick as the forest was opened up to farmland, just as soon as there were increased edges and more opportunity, then the deer of that region began to see intruders and interlopers from out west. At first, understandably, there was stiff resistance by the local matriarchs, but when the farmland kept blossoming, when the harsh forests of the east gave way to sun and clover, then the strangers were able to horn their way in, especially if they offered something more than competition.

It didn't take long before alliances between the interlopers and the various local deer dynasties sprang up. This was not necessarily a given, not right away at least. The deer of the eastern corridor had suffered greatly during the ice age. They had been driven far south and hard against the coast lines.

The deer in the middle of the country had it much easier. All they had to do was bend and give way to the ice. When the glaciers finally receded, the deer simply followed them north as they maintained their normal life. Thus, the descendants of Scipio were able to blend in relatively easily with the resident herds of that area. This was not the case in the east before the coming of the white man.

The glaciers in the east had been thick and had scraped off the tops of the mountains. When they retreated, the forest was dense and the river valleys were narrow. The further north you went, the more boreal in nature the woodland became with large stands of spruce and fir. A home for the few but not for many. Resistance to newcomers was fierce. The only thing which could overcome this resistance was a lack of something. Nature abhors a vacuum but also finds a lack of something almost as detestable. A lack of water, a lack of food, a lack of genetic diversity will overcome almost any prejudice if these conditions threaten to help create a vacuum. The deer of the east were tough, they were paranoid, self-reliant and desperately in need of an infusion of new blood. The descendants of Scipio fit the bill beautifully.

Once the word got out in the white-tail world that there was a new opportunity developing in the east, then the wandering gene awoke. The ice circle which had held it in place broke apart before the floodwaters of instinct and courage. The does took off. They meandered through southern Pennsylvania, crossed the Delaware River, and headed up the east coast.

By the time the Civil War had ended, they had gotten lazy again, however. The wandering gene had kicked back into its cold, circular vacation. There were more people than ever, and the deer adapted to them. They, the deer, kept to the swamps, to the edges, to the places that the people didn't want, and they prospered. Every spring they would have two or three fawns and their numbers grew. But the colder winters to the north in Maine brought back unwelcome, ancestral memories. Most of the deer were in no hurry to rush up there. But there was, nevertheless, a lack up there, and there was also a lack in southern New England. There was an opportunity developing up in Maine just as a window was closing down below. In short, the activity of humans had increased the deer population in the south, while the brutal winters in Maine had kept the deer herd thin.

For a while, the bucks coming from the Scipio line had done well in the area around Massachusetts. Probably they still are, as far as anyone knows. But the does were restless once the numbers got up. As the farms and small towns grew in southern and western Maine, the does chose to ignore the Maine winters and they headed north. By the early 1900s the first descendants of Scipio were around Portland.

–CHAPTER 3–

For the vast majority of his life, Essene had lived within a relatively small home range, perhaps five or six square miles. Freely giving in to an unrestrained, natural tendency toward an unreasonable paranoia, he sought out thick cover wherever he went. It just so happened that the tangled, huge swamp that served as his core area was an important junction of the white-tail world, where the coastal plains ended, and the foothills of western Maine began. This circumstance attracted all sorts of characters, good and bad.

For a dominant buck like Essene, this situation was ideal if he lived long enough, and that was easier said than done. When he was two years old, he started to feel his oats and promptly proceeded to ram around with the intention of partaking of the white-tail cornucopia exploding all around him. But there were plenty of big bucks around and it wasn't long before he was put in his place.

Luckily for him, Essene was as intelligent as he was big. It didn't take but a couple of applications of what constituted proper decorum for Essene to steer clear of dangerous activity. He wasn't ready for prime time and he knew it. In fact, he had enough instinct for self-preservation to understand that the time to assert himself in that crowded region was at least a year or so away. Still, at age three he was not going to allow himself to be kept completely out of the picture.

Fortunately for him a situation developed during the very earliest part of the rut in September which saved his self-esteem, if not his life. His territory was to be the main battlefield for two master bucks of the first order who had traveled great distances to settle a long-standing dispute between them. Anybody who was foolish enough to get in the way would promptly be reduced to toast.

Well, lo and behold, about that time Essene sensed a great vacuum to the south. Fighting all his training and all his instincts, Essene soon demonstrated the sort of flexibility which would soon make him one of the best master bucks of all time. Giving way to the inevitable, Essene, for one year and one year only, forsook his home territory and took a long sojourn to the south, braving strange ground and unknown adversaries with a single-mindedness which his innermost heart understood only very vaguely.

On the surface, Servilia was pretty much an average individual, though perhaps a bit taller and broader through the chest than is considered normal. Growing up in the area south of Portland, she seemed content with being a deer of the suburbs. She hung around all the fashionable crossings, ran away from and toward the sleek, well-groomed bucks of that neighborhood, while having two sets of two fawns before cutting back to a solitary fawn in her third year. She seemed well entrenched in that cool Scipio circle as she approached the zenith of her reproductive life. Then, at the end of that third summer, a gentle, northerly breeze jarred her from her complacency.

At that moment her long dormant wandering gene abruptly kicked in, and she promptly bid adieu to the group she had spent her entire life with. She didn't go a huge distance, but it was far enough so that she never saw her immediate family again, other than the fawn who had come along with her. That fawn, a doe, would take off in full Scipio earnest the next year.

Somewhere north of Gray, just as the western foothills were faintly appearing through the heavy summer haze, Servilia found a gap in the local populations and promptly set up camp. Her fawn, understandably nervous and anxious at being separated from her relatives and playmates, clung to her mother's side and persisted in nudging Servilia from time to time. Finally, Servilia pinned back her ears and laid down the law severely enough to convince the fawn that further protests were futile. Possibly this is what convinced the fawn to take off on a long, one-way journey the following year. Sometimes it didn't take a lot to trigger the wandering gene once an individual was sufficiently removed from the circle of ice, the comfort zone which sometimes held the clan of Scipio together for generations.

Servilia herself felt a presence of potentials but not the potential for further wandering. She had gone as far as she would ever go. If anything, she would drift back toward her former circle as the years went by, but not all at once. She was at the mercy, not of one trigger, not of one genetic impulse or inevitability, but at the mercy of several gears and triggers which time had chosen for her to express and expose to the outside world. Her uncharacteristic display of irritation toward this year's fawn was a sign that all the genetic ducks were starting to get in a row. Everything that she apparently was: ordinary, unsubstantial, or otherwise mundane, all of that would be revealed to be, if not a lie, then at the very least a clever, natural act of deferred gratification.

This was a very unique way for a superior individual like Scipio to fix an indelible, and necessary, stamp on his kind. Servilia was a very reliable mother but nothing special, at least on the outside. She was not too big, and she was not too small. There was nothing overtly unique about her that would draw the attention of predators. She blended in with the herd. She was an extraordinarily average serving of deer porridge, which was more than enough to get her here where it mattered. In short, Servilia was a vessel of the best type: unaware, yet capable and deserving. The roulette wheel of her powerful lineage had been clicking for centuries, and when that clicking stopped, her number had come up. An important part of the power, size and intelligence of Scipio had been held in reserve for a special moment. Now, with a dreadful kind of anxiety, Servilia faced that moment with a confused courage which continued to alter her inner makeup.

At first, she languished in her new surroundings. She ate feebly and ignored the promptings of her fawn to play and to explore. Then the appearance of goldenrod at the edges of nearby fields gently nudged her from her lethargic state. Fall was coming. For the sake of her current fawn and for the sake of the one to come, Servilia realized that she needed to familiarize herself more thoroughly with her new home. She might not be here forever, but she was going to be here for a while. She needed to find out where the water was, where the swamps, fields, soft and hardwood stands were. And what about the predators? Where did the coydogs like to swing through? How often did they make their rounds over their territories?

At best, obtaining that knowledge was an inexact science, but an attempt had to be made to come up with a good consistent guess. A deer living with a group of related, or otherwise reliable companions, stood a good chance of keeping the coydogs in one area of the forest, while the deer would be residing in another part. Many eyes and ears made light work of this problem most of the time. Skittish behavior on the part of non-lethal denizens of the forest who happened to be hanging around was enough to put the whole herd on high alert. A critter running was enough to get the deer moving in an oblique direction to the path taken by the fox, raccoon, grouse, turkey or whatever was hightailing out of the neighborhood at the time.

In order to set up shop in a new territory, Servilia had had to locate a vacuum in the adjacent territories of two nearby matriarchs. She was now an adult and had acquired a thorough understanding of proper deer etiquette. During the next week or so she gently probed the boundaries of these two matriarchs. It wouldn't take very long to figure out which of the two would be more tolerant of her and her fawn as long as they stayed on the outskirts of that particular doe's domain.

Now Servilia had the aid of that group's eyes and ears when coydogs would begin to approach them with bad intent. It would take but a short while before Servilia could establish a rough estimate as to when this particular enemy might be coming. Though deer always had to be vigilant, nevertheless, in warmer months, they could use these rough estimates to relax and rest somewhat while they gained weight and strength for the cold winter when the coydogs would be hunting them in earnest.

Soon this particular family began to appreciate

Servilia's presence. She was intelligent and not aggressive. As long as she didn't compete or otherwise pose a threat to their territorial imperative, then she and her fawn were readily accepted. Besides, maybe there were good reasons for her being here. Perhaps her relationship with them would strengthen their own genetic line in the future. Stranger things had happened in the past. And there was the fact that this group lived in a land of plenty, so she and her fawn were left alone.

Once all this was apparent to Servilia, she then set out to learn one more thing. When the coydogs got too thick or had successfully snuck up on them in the rain and fog, then the deer would have to resort to desperate measures. There were fields and roads all around here. It was time to ascertain where the shin-fa, the "shiny faced ones," lived. Knowing where the nearest humans lived and how to get close to either them or their dwellings was crucial in times of heavy coydog infestation.

This tactic could be a double-edged sword. During the fall, if you got too close, the shin-fa were apt to emerge from their giant, turtle-shell dwellings with the dreaded black horn that deer understood needed to be feared as much as the coydogs, maybe more. If the snow was deep or a thin crust held up the coydogs as they closed in on the heels of the fleeing deer, then there was no choice. The thunder of the moveable black horn was preferable to the snarling sharp fangs of the coydog. Many times, if the coydogs were careless or sufficiently driven by the pangs of hunger, it would be the coydogs who died by the hands of the shin-fa and not the deer.

But those were rare instances. Usually just being around the places of the shin-fa was enough to keep the coydogs honest. It wasn't just the black horns which gave them pause, it was the presence of big domestic dogs that had to be considered as well. Deer also had to be careful of the dogs but if the dogs were well trained or otherwise restrained, then the deer could rush by them and set them to barking. The coydogs had learned over the years that once the dogs got to barking, the shin-fa were apt to appear soon after. Running deer were a sign to them to break out the black horns.

Mainly though, the entire effort was to buy some time. Very rarely did the shin-fa actually shoot coydogs as a result of deer activity. Once in a while the shin-fa might see deer moving along nearby in a manner which suggested that they were being pursued. A shot back into the woods in the direction from which the deer had just run would be all that was required. Any coydog chasing the deer would have to readjust their hunt, and that would be all it took to give the deer time to escape. Usually just being around the general vicinity of the shin-fa was enough to create some elbow room between the deer and the coydogs.

Besides protection, the shin-fa also provided food of one type or another. In late summer or early fall the gardens of the shin-fa would offer up a highly nutritious and beneficial addition to the wild food that deer generally survived on. With the rut fast approaching, it was very important to get some high-octane reserves in place for the demanding times ahead. The ends of blackberry bushes were okay, but a row of string beans all laid out in smorgasbord fashion was a much more sensible alternative for deer getting ready to rock and roll.

Apples were great also. The shin-fa always seemed to have more than they needed. In fact, frequently the ground beneath the trees would literally be covered with the unused fruit. This was especially true of the orchards which had recently been overtaken by the forest. In this area most of the apple trees were on the edge of lawns, but not all of them. There were still a few old run-down farms around. On the end of one of the few remaining hay fields near where Servilia lived was an actual orchard which had only recently been surrounded by young pine and gray birch. It only contained eight trees. However, it nevertheless held a lot of food in good years, and, more importantly, Servilia could get to it easily from that part of the surrounding forest where she had decided to spend most of her time.

After she had located the orchard, she and her fawn then took a few days to map out some safe routes through the area. When that was accomplished to her satisfaction, she then proceeded to locate the most convenient and bountiful gardens before heading back to the safety of the forest to wait. What exactly they were waiting for even Servilia didn't have much of a notion. The fawn, of course, was completely in the dark, but Servilia, in the way of her kind, vaguely understood that something was about to happen or to be revealed.

—CHAPTER 4—

Essene had not intended to go very far. After all, at three years of age he was nowhere near his prime and therefore unprepared for being a "line buck." That, being a line buck, happened when a truly dominant buck was at or near the height of his physical prowess so that the rigors and demands of intruding onto other big bucks' territories could be successfully pulled off. It never did any good to go barging into someone else's bedroom if you were going to have some unmentionable part of your anatomy handed to you.

But staying put on his home turf that particular year wasn't going to work out very well for him. With two dominant master bucks jockeying for an ultimate showdown, Essene would have been little more than target practice. His future potential was more than evident in terms of body and antler size, but if he had made the mistake of challenging either of the two fellows invading his territory that fall then his story could well have been short and not very sweet.

Besides, even if he wasn't physically injured by one of the invading brutes, his dignity and self-esteem nevertheless could have suffered irreversible damage. That sort of thing could be sensed by bucks in rut, and it could have led to unnecessary fighting in the future. Excessive fighting during the rut can lead to a state of exhaustion that could cause a buck not to survive a winter.

Essene, showing a trait which would serve him well in the years to come, gave way to an outbreak of common sense. He would leave the field of battle to his superior foes, let them impregnate the local does with absurdly desirable genes, and then come back to reap the benefits of their considerable efforts when he was a year older and much more able to take care of himself.

Hopefully, his older foes would also be much more the worse for wear at that point, if they ever did come around there again. Chances are they would never return to that place. A master buck sometimes had a huge kingdom to tend to. More often than not, a truly dominant animal might only pass through a certain territory but once in his lifetime.

Essene was sort of gambling on this to be the case in this instance. Besides, there was something else afoot. He sensed a vacuum to his south, and, being an unusually intelligent buck, he wisely started to follow the path of least resistance around the end of August. It was a lovely vacation with only a few of the local bucks raising an eyebrow as he lumbered past. It wasn't anywhere near the rut yet. A couple of times he stopped and actually jousted playfully with some of the local bachelor bucks to give them fair warning as to what was what. He was not in his prime, but he was still a force to be reckoned with. When the time came to retreat to his home territory, Essene wanted to be a known quantity. He didn't want to have to fight his way home. Most of these young bucks would readily give way now that they had tested each other a little.

So, gradually the leaves in the lowlands began to change color, and the light began to have a shallow quality to it. The bachelor groups disbursed, and the time of playfulness came to an end. Essene lingered no longer than he had to in any given area. He followed the path of least resistance and he did so with an increasing urgency and speed. The places of vacuum between territories sucked him along, until the mountains overlooking his core area were barely visible in the distance. Then one day, he slowed down and prepared for the rut proper. He had gone as far as he needed to.

As with everything else about her, the time that Servilia usually came into heat was about average. She was never early, never late. When all the other does in her vicinity were in the middle of their cyclical eruptions, Servilia was right there amongst them making her contribution to the seasonal commotion. When a decent buck came along, she and her extended family would lay out the welcome mat, and the games would begin. The emphasis for her had always been to blend in, to never stand out, nor to draw unnecessary attention to herself. For her to now be in this isolated condition was very bewildering for her. She had not been driven off by a jealous aunt or an aggressive sister. She had been a good team player within her old group, but now, inexplicably, she was a team of one. All of her life she had been average in every respect, but now, somewhat surprisingly, she discovered that she possessed an extraordinary amount of courage, the way individuals sometimes do when placed in situations of uncommon stress.

When the matriarch, who had earlier that summer allowed Servilia and her fawn to partake of the protection of the larger group, began to display the body language of annoyance as the rut approached, Servilia wisely withdrew into a state of even greater isolation then she had previously existed in. Still, something had drawn her here. All the elements that had gone into her making, over the recent centuries, were now locked behind the tension of a hairspring trigger. The apparently normal geodes which had formerly contained the rigid forms of her genetic makeup had begun to melt slightly and reconstruct themselves as she waited, with no small amount of trepidation, waited for something to happen.

She moved her fawn aside one morning and went off a little by herself. No, she had never been an early breeder, but as she rounded the bend of a trail there was a flicker of movement coming toward her through some heavy brush. Instantly, things started to loosen and flow. When Essene rounded into view with his great antlers down in passionate aggression, Servilia was suddenly completely awash in her heat. It was the only time this had ever happened to her like this, and it never would be so again. But once was enough.

It was a peculiar episode for Essene also. Until that moment his neck was scarcely beginning to show the signs of swelling which always came with the rut. After all, it was barely past the middle of September. By the time he and Servilia had completed their time of breeding, however, his neck had swollen bigger than it had ever been in his brief lifetime. In between the frenzied bouts of breeding Essene was thrashing a lot of good-sized trees and tearing up the countryside in general. A local buck, curious as to what all the commotion was about, came round to investigate and was promptly whipped in good fashion. Perhaps if he had been in full rut himself, he might have offered some real resistance to Essene's violence. Luckily for him, however, he got the message in a hurry and proceeded to spread the word around the immediate neighborhood.

Shortly thereafter, Servilia was kind enough to steer Essene toward the matriarch who had befriended she and her fawn earlier that summer. Essene had the same effect on this matriarch that he had had on Servilia. For this act of unintentional kindness, Servilia was thereby granted a much more secure position within that matriarch's group. At what was to prove to be the most vital point in her life, Servilia was a team player once more.

The fawn that she would have the following spring would have the security of numbers to help in assuring his survival. The group seemed to recognize that the arrival of Essene increased their overall chances of succeeding in the white-tail world. But the best seed had gone to the first. Essene would go all around the surrounding countryside that fall, and he brought forth some glorious fruit from the worthy and the unworthy alike. But none of the many fawns attributed to him were anywhere near the equal of what he and Servilia produced. None of them compared to Nethanel.

At a very early age it occurred to Nethanel that his mother had something very specific in mind for him. Gently at first, then much more persistently, she was frequently steering him away from the local herd of deer. She directed his attention to the ancient paths leading away to the north. In a short while, even his sister was not encouraged to follow him and their mother on what would become daily excursions to the outer limits of their current territory. They were following the way Essene had disappeared the fall before. They kept going back in that direction, not every day, but frequently.

Finally, Servilia seemed to gain confidence in what she was doing. She located a path which led up to the summit of a narrow, rounded hill. The hill was overlooking a substantial swamp but that wasn't what drew her up here. Just off to their right, at the very apex of the knoll was a thin line of young, scrubby hemlock. Two of those hemlock were far enough apart to form a dark gateway to a grassy opening before the hill dropped back down into the edge of the swamp. Servilia slowly eased through this gateway and then stopped, looking northward as she did so. Her attitude, her posture, commanded Nethanel to come forward and to stand by her right shoulder. Once he got there, he followed her line of vision to determine what she was looking at. Through some ice-damaged maples, some twenty or thirty miles distant, a mountain range was visible. There was a slight breeze that day, and some fair-weather clouds were playing back and forth both near and far.

Suddenly, a gentle shift in that wind far away focused the sharp sunlight somewhere beyond the row of mountains that they had originally been looking at and revealed a deeper, more distant range of mountains. Body language means more to some species then to others. With deer it means a lot. When those deeper, far away range of mountains came into view, Servilia tensed noticeably. In doing so she intentionally set off a sort of lateral line, a neuromas, which deer used in much the same way a school of fish use their mechano-receptive organs to detect prey, or a predator, to determine the direction and speed that school will head to or away from. With that very simple movement from his mother, Nethanel instantaneously knew where his future lay. All he had to do was get there.

–CHAPTER 5–
Crassus

Not too far north of where Nethanel and his mother had stood that day, began the vast territory of Crassus. It stretched up over halfway toward the first substantial foothills before a small, deep river served as a convenient, though somewhat arbitrary, border on the northern side. The eastern and western limits of his domain, as well as the southern border, were defined by highways which eventually made a great, rough circle when connected with the deep river. Of course, none of that really mattered. Crassus went where he wanted, when the mood was upon him. However, that fifteen square mile Ponderosa suited him just fine most of the time. It was an area chock full of fields, swamp and water that provided him with a deer heaven that could scarcely be improved on even in his wildest dreams.

Crassus had a lot of wild dreams. He knew

where all the best abandoned farms were, and it was near them that he would leave one of his infrequent rubs. Where he chose to leave his rubs was done very carefully in a crafty, stealthy way. He would find a knoll only slightly higher than the rest of the surrounding terrain and choose the tree there that mattered. It didn't necessarily have to be a big tree, but, as was usual with his kind, bigger was always better. A large tree rubbed in the proper manner and facing the right way would act like a great beacon, alternately warning or welcoming bucks or does respectively for a surprisingly long distance sometimes. If done properly—and his always were—a deer descending down a slope a quarter mile away could look across a swamp and catch all the latest news as Crassus saw it.

When the apples from certain abandoned apple trees had fallen to the ground and had fermented long enough, the whole deer population in that general vicinity knew about it. It was party time in a truly hedonistic fashion, and everybody was invited, provided they didn't have antlers. From these few, special apple trees, a great network of extremely isolated rubs was spread over a huge territory to let every buck know where they stood in the regional pecking order. If anyone had a problem with that, then the bucks knew where to find him.

The core area that Crassus used for his autumn bedroom wasn't squarely in these abandoned orchards, but it wasn't far from them either. The rubs he left by these potent apples could lead a buck right up to Crassus' pillow if that's what they really desired. In fact, every once in a while, a large buck might stumble onto a batch of Crassus' favorite fermented apples, sample a few, and then get it into their rut infested heads to pester the old boy on his own turf.

If they were lucky, Crassus would be off ramming around at the further ends of his domain, and therefore they could, once sobering up the next morning, depart from his kingdom with the delusion of grandeur that somehow involved them kicking in the door of the great master's bedroom and taking the best does for themselves. Usually however, once the effects of the fermented apples wore off, most of these animals were intelligent enough to leave well enough alone, and they never returned to that place a second time.

Crassus himself was pragmatic about the whole process. When he was out and about determining which important matriarchs were in or close to being in heat, an up and coming regional buck might see fit to at least put up a show of resistance to mollify an injured ego. Crassus loved the big life, not the fighting life. He could love and leave with the best of them with no hard feelings whatsoever when the time of departure was at hand. He didn't bear any of these subordinate bucks any real ill will as long as they didn't take themselves too seriously. What fighting that occurred between he and them in their "home" territory was for educational purposes only. It was all for exercise and for artistic expression. Only occasionally did a buck from his home turf have the poor taste to dig in and do battle in earnest. Crassus would take care of these unfortunate pretenders as though he were picking his teeth after a good meal. If they persisted in their obnoxious behavior, then Crassus was capable of meting out a dose of severe punishment. The worst of these offenders were ushered off the premises with the help of a stout hoof and a sharp horn. They were sent into exile with no hope of ever returning. Crassus did not forget nor forgive. They would have to find new territory elsewhere or else face the real wrath of Crassus in any return match.

Crassus was intelligent in that way. His real

violence was reserved for those who actually earned it, not these local yokels. It was an honest sort of threat that brought out his best. When the massive animals from the outlying districts decided to take him on, they never were able to fully appreciate the elements which Crassus was able to marshal up against them. He always had a small, decisive moment of surprise working for him it seemed.

No deer ever snuck up on him. He had spies everywhere. Like any sensible aristocrat, Crassus had a generous population of sniveling underlings who, at the first sighting of a dangerous opponent, would hastily flee from that intruder and, in doing so, would unintentionally stir up the necessary amount of usually innocent bystanders to eventually alert Crassus who, more often than not, would apt to be picking his teeth in his inner sanctum as the intruder approached. He didn't believe in fretting or otherwise wasting valuable energy. There would be no great demonstrations nor undue shows of false bravado. Understatement had always suited him just fine.

It didn't really matter whether the intruder arrived unannounced or not. When it came to fighting, Crassus had a game plan, and he always stuck with it as closely as he could. He was a massive animal. Always fond of eating copiously, he could almost be accused of being pudgy, which is unusual for a white-tail deer. His live weight was always well north of three hundred pounds. But he carried that weight deceptively. His shoulders and rear quarters were abnormally wide, though perfectly distributed to conceal their deadly potential. He was slightly shorter than normal which accentuated his pudgy appearance much more then would have otherwise been the case if his height had been normal or above average. With his extended stomach reaching down toward the ground as a result of all his copious eating, one could almost understand why some of his rivals initially underestimated what he was all about. However, the smarter challengers were able to take one glance at Crassus and come to a quick appreciation as to what they were about to undertake.

It was his antlers which gave them pause. They were a distinctly nasty piece of work. Nastier than any of them had ever seen. Sometimes just the sight of them was enough to turn would-be challengers into shallow shells of their former selves. More often than not Crassus would frequently chase after these cowardly types as they fled. The weakness they displayed disgusted him and aroused a desire to rid the white-tailed race of their dangerous failing. But he wouldn't waste a lot of his precious energy in this manner. And, although he would eventually be content to let the unworthy bucks run off unmolested, he never allowed the brave ones to escape unscathed. Any individual who had the audacity to come for blood usually tasted plenty of his own when he finished his struggles with Crassus, if he was lucky.

The antlers of Crassus were a multifaceted tool which he had learned to wield with an unmerciful efficiency. At first glance, they appeared to be a somewhat typical swamp buck rack with the large, heavy tines, sweeping protectively and majestically over the front of his slightly graying face. At their base, his antlers were well over six inches in circumference, and they appeared to blossom from there. The main beams looked to be too heavy for the bases to support as they made their way high over his head before curving gracefully toward each other at their decidedly pointed ends. In places, where the longer tines were, the beams of his antlers would approach eight inches in diameter, though they would be quite slender at their tops where the tines erupted from them. Not surprisingly, on the whole, the tines of these antlers were proportional to their base and beam. That is, all except for one.

On what would be the left side of Crassus, the G-2 tine of that antler was truly remarkable. While all the other tines were long, massive and impressive, conforming nicely to the overall template created by the swamp rack model, the G-2 tine on the left-hand side stood out, almost literally, like a sore thumb. It was three inches longer and twice as big around as the corresponding G-2 tine on the right-hand side of Crassus' rack. And, while all the other tines curved gracefully and obediently forward the way you might expect them to, this left-hand tine, on the other hand, pointed straight up and slightly outward from the beam when Crassus had his head lowered for battle.

At first glance, one would expect this tine to be used for a thrusting action, like a spear. However, while that would be true later on once a fight had been decided, the real function that Crassus had adopted for this aberrant tine was more clever and devious than that of a common spear.

Going into a fight, any experienced buck would see the obvious dangers that this particular tine posed, and they would then take the appropriate measures to guard against these dangers. They would consciously build their fight around this tine and direct all their energy toward dealing with the force that Crassus directed along this point.

If possible, Crassus did everything he could to set the stage for the fight to go in this direction. Once he understood that an adversary was lurking in the immediate vicinity, he would then attempt to use his intimate knowledge of his home territory to make the fight as quick and painless as possible. If he caught a glimpse of his opponent heading toward him, Crassus would locate a small depression in the ground. Standing in this depression, Crassus would appear to be shorter or smaller than he actually was. If he was caught off guard and couldn't accomplish that particular deception, then he would just get behind some small trees or appropriately sized rocks that he would, with great skill, use to pull off a deception. He also tried to get some low brush in front of him to break up the profile of his rack. In short, Crassus would do anything he could to ensure that his opponent was not psychologically prepared to deal with what he was about to endure.

Some bucks made a big deal of showing off everything they had, like the "cowboy walk" of male bears, in an effort to avoid an imminent battle. Crassus, on the other hand, was a total pragmatic when it came to someone trying to influence his territorial imperative. When a dominant buck presented himself to Crassus, Crassus never once gave a thought to avoiding a fight. On the contrary, once an intruder had the poor taste to show up, spoiling for a fight on his doorstep, then Crassus would use every bit of his intelligence to bring the fight on and to conduct that fight on his terms only. Many bucks didn't expect this, and this was why Crassus was so successful.

From the very beginning of any conflict, Crassus did everything he could to dictate the direction that the conflict would take. He would try to establish an uphill position, keep a tree or rock to his backside to provide additional balance or power to push off from if it seemed to his advantage to do so, and, most importantly of all, he made doubly sure that his opponent became completely aware of an oversized G-2 tine waving around somewhere uncomfortably close to the front of his face. Like any good boxer, Crassus would jab and thrust with the accursed tine and then come around with the right side of his rack, probing and moving, looking for weaknesses before setting up his opponent for future punishment. If an opponent chose to stand pat directly in front of him, then Crassus would proceed to jab and drive the wayward tine toward an eye or nose. This usually had the desired effect.

Under this circumstance, a foe would have no choice but to attempt to use his own antlers to slow down or otherwise ward off the thrusting action of the malignant tine. They would try to seize, or otherwise maintain, a strong contact with the dangerous weapon probing toward them. Crassus would be calmly waiting for this eventuality. Then, when he sensed his opponent's center of balance was properly placed in a perfect alignment along his inner fulcrum, Crassus would proceed to unveil the real purpose of his big G-2 tine. At a crucial moment, which Crassus, through long and ruthless practice had learned to identify instantaneously, Crassus would flick his big tine and cause his opponent to lose his balance. Even if the opponent lost his balance only a little bit, it would be too much. Surging forward, Crassus would risk everything at this point, and once an opponent felt even the beginning of the tine starting to make contact with flesh and bone, then the contest was usually decided as discretion, in most cases, quickly became the better part of valor.

If this wasn't the case, if an opponent unwisely decided to struggle on, then the punishment handed out by Crassus would be severe indeed. Once the tine was freed up, it was always better if the opponent ran away. A couple of times stubborn opponents were nearly killed outright. And even if they weren't severely injured physically, all who lingered imprudently in front of Crassus were never quite the same afterwards. They would be cast into an exile understood by all. At the age of eight years, Crassus ruled his empire with an iron tine.

–CHAPTER 6–

When Crassus was eight, Nethanel was seven. A prolific breeder, Nethanel had wobbled slightly to the southwest of his birthplace in his earlier years and had produced many healthy but otherwise undistinguished offspring. Perhaps taking a cue from his mother, the young who had sprung from his loins were very average in size and temperament, so far.

This could be regarded as being a rather strange result, because Nethanel was an extraordinary buck. At first glance this might not be readily evident because he carried himself with a frame which was perfectly proportional in every respect. He was tall enough and long enough to disguise the extent of his overall mass. The fact of the matter was, however, that Nethanel was the heaviest deer in the northeast. At this time in his life when he was onto his feed just ahead of the rut, he would fluctuate somewhere between three hundred and twenty-five to three hundred and fifty pounds. Basically, he was a huge Ontario deer who had just happened to land in Maine.

He was so big in fact that his mother had actually had a difficult time birthing him. But she was a capable, resourceful individual, and eventually she was able to deposit him on the cold April ground. After that, everything more or less went according to schedule. At two years of age he left the resident bachelor group and had been on his own ever since, except of course in the winter where numbers were needed to tramp down snow and help watch for coydogs.

Because of his size, he became a somewhat lethargic individual. He wasn't dull nor dim witted, but due to the lack of any real competition, he could almost be described as bored. He sensed that he was not where he was supposed to be. As he began to approach his prime, this sense of unfulfillment caused him to lose the velvet on his antlers in an increasingly violent manner as each year went past.

Nethanel had deceptive antlers. They appeared smaller than they actually were. Indeed, if they had grown in a more direct proportion to his body size, then he might have starved to death trying to gather enough sustenance to grow them every year. They were still huge, but they just didn't look that huge on him. Although his father, Essene, a dominant buck, had sported a true swamp rack, Nethanel had drawn from his mother's side of the family. The strongest part of her had come to hail from the Ohio region. Therefore, he had a more open rack than his father had, though it still had a small sweep toward the front of his face. He had a twenty-six inch inside spread, balanced along a handsome, eleven-point rack. The beams at their bases were seven inches in circumference. These beams were nine inches around just before the G-2 tines, which were of a proportional height to the rest of the rack—around eleven inches. And, while this rack, at first glance, might have appeared somewhat mundane to us, other bucks saw things as they were. This was especially true when the time came to challenge Nethanel on the field of battle. When things got up close and personal, frequently, all Nethanel saw of his opponents were their rear ends as they literally and unceremoniously headed for the hills.

Because of this sort of reaction, it wasn't long before Nethanel had left all the genetic footprint that he was going to in this particular area. So, out of necessity almost, he was soon thinking about heading for the hills himself. Because of the imprinting that his mother had seen fit to bestow upon him, he had always had an inclination to strike out in that direction anyway. More and more as his early years had begun to give way to his middle ones; more and more Nethanel would find himself gazing off toward those distant mountains and feel a deep disquiet with his current circumstances. All he needed was a gentle push, and he would gladly be ready to vamoose.

That push came in the fall of his seventh year. Like all deer of his magnitude, his mother had subjected him to an extremely arduous and thorough preparation for avoiding predators. This was especially true for staying away from the shin-fa in the fall. Servilia was a normal doe in many respects, but with the birth of Nethanel, there came within her an increased awareness and awakening of a need and ability to properly oversee the education of her most important son.

She had always been a good mother but, without a doubt, the undeniable presence and impetus of Essene's genetic input played a big part in her heightened maternal awareness. Yes, Servilia did an admirable job, but there was only so much she could do because the shin-fa were a malignant bunch. Morning, noon and night they laid their traps, took pictures with trail cameras, and did everything they could, legal and otherwise, to harvest the best that the white-tail race had to offer. In snow, sleet and freezing rain, they remorselessly pursued Nethanel and his kind. But in spite of all this, at seven years of age Nethanel had come to the conclusion that he had the shin-fa all figured out. This complacency would propel him to his greatest lessons.

Rail had been forced to attend a sister-in-law's favorite uncle's wedding anniversary. He had fought hard to get himself excused from the festivities, but in the end, common sense and an offer from his sister-in-law's husband to get in some hunting that morning ahead of the celebration, had soothed the pain of missing the second Saturday of the deer season.

The ground chosen for him to hunt showed promise and had guaranteed a safe return for noontime, when they would have to get out of the woods and go to the party. It was a big piece of land, but he was given good directions and ended up where he was supposed to meet his sister-in-law's husband. He was a bit early so while he waited for his partner to show up, he found a dry stump to sit on and had a brief snack of trail mix.

This particular section of woodland had been cut hard some dozen years before. The stump he sat on was on the corner of a twitch road which ran down a long gentle slope in front of him. This twitch road gave him a somewhat open view of about seventy-five yards. On either side of the road, the saplings, trying to reclaim the cut-off, offered only small, imperfect openings that Rail could see through. As it was the middle of the day, Rail wasn't expecting anything to happen. He was just waiting for his hunting partner to show up, and, considering the dense vegetation around him, this was as good as any place to hang around at.

Once he finished his snack, he settled down to wait in earnest. He remained perfectly motionless and watched down the twitch road, emphasizing on the woods to the right of the road, where he expected his sister-in-law's husband to emerge from. The deer came from the left and fifteen yards further down the hill than the place he had been concentrating on. The deer wasn't running, just moving along at a steady pace, but before Rail had a chance to react, the deer was across the road and back into the brush.

Rail had one brief glimpse of the buck's tremendous rack. He snapped off his safety, got his elbows to his knees and proceeded to follow the deer as best he could through the heavy brush. He watched the abbreviated movements of the buck, sneaking with great purpose through a dense thicket of young beech trees which had most of their rusty leaves still attached. While peering intensely through his scope, Rail would occasionally look quickly around the right edge of it to see if he could determine whether or not that there were any openings that the deer might be moving through. He could see that there was only one small slab of clean air that the buck seemed to be moving toward. However, just before he moved into that small opening, the deer stopped.

Rail had been here before. The top of his left knee was starting to pain him some from the pressure that his sharp left elbow was exerting on it, as the heavy gun began to sway ever so slightly as a result of the lengthy wait. Rail didn't worry about the swaying gun. He knew he could tighten up when the time came. He just hoped his hunting buddy didn't come blundering along and jump the deer into the next county. His luck held and the deer moved slowly forward. The swaying stopped.

A front leg and a reasonable amount of shoulder showed up in the small, clear spot. There was a small smattering of beech leaves covering the place where an effective shot would have to go. Rail felt he had to gamble. He put the cross hairs where he felt they needed to be, put his finger on the trigger, and slowly began to exhale, waiting for the sound of the rifle going off before he even realized that he had squeezed the trigger.

Nethanel had been becoming annoyed. All morning long this shin-fa had been dogging him. Ordinarily with such thick cover to work with and no snow on the ground, getting rid of an idiot such as the shin-fa following him would have been no problem whatsoever. A few steps to the side, a little courage and patience, and pretty soon the would-be killer would be well past and on his way to another failed hunt.

However, it soon dawned on Nethanel that this shin-fa was no dub. Moreover, what made the situation even more troubling was the fact that he had never experienced any danger whatsoever in this area before. They were in a big bowl, with the tangled clear-cut surrounding a large, similarly tangled cedar swamp. Nethanel had just moved in here to escape some unusually heavy hunting pressure on the outside. To announce his happy arrival to the resident does, and to any would-be rivals, he had chosen a large poplar tree which had grown on a small plateau that overlooked the end of the swamp and had relieved it of its bark. Nethanel now recognized this as potentially being a mistake. That rub, despite being made in what he had considered a safe territory, had shined like a huge beacon to anyone who came near it, including the hateful shin-fa who was now causing him so much displeasure.

Going forever in half circles, then back-tracking with no apparent rhyme nor reason, first with the wind in his face, then sideways into it, and more often than not, allowing the prevailing breeze to carry his offensive scent far out ahead of him to let Nethanel know exactly where he was, the shin-fa cast his patient web and wove a deep fabric of doubt into Nethanel's mind. At times, the hunter would sneak ahead in super stealth mode, peering intently into the thickest brush before coming to a complete halt for long, tense minutes. Then, without any apparent reason, he would walk quickly and nosily up over the end of a nearby knoll, crashing and thrashing wildly as if almost running before the deadly silence would break out again.

Nethanel knew that he should not, could not, run. But this hunter was not going to give up. How he knew this, Nethanel couldn't imagine, nor did he particularly care. He just knew that the hunter almost had him pegged, almost had him figured out, and that this hunter was willing to commit as much time as necessary to force Nethanel into making a fatal mistake.

Nethanel waited for the man's scent to come strongly to him one more time, and then the big buck made his move. With a soft bound into a nearby stand of young fir, he then set out with a fast walk which was not going to end until he was absolutely certain that he would never come into contact with this particular shin-fa again. All was going well until he came to the twitch road that Rail was sitting on.

In this close cover, the twitch road represented an opening, an opportunity, for his enemies to see him. By old habit and good training, Nethanel went across the road in a measured manner, which he hoped would not draw the attention of any shin-fa who might happen to be in the area. If the opening had been larger, he would have speeded up or even jumped over the road, but, though he was seen, the strategy worked. He had not been seen by Rail until it was apparently too late.

Still, almost instantly upon entering the road, Nethanel suspected that something was wrong. Even while in motion going through the thick brush, Nethanel detected a brief, shining moment as Rail picked up his gun and prepared to shoot. Though safe in his motionless state, Nethanel knew he couldn't remain frozen where he was forever. The shin-fa who had been chasing him all morning was somewhere nearby. Nethanel had to move, but he opted to sneak because he wasn't certain what was above him on the twitch road. If it was a shin-fa, perhaps he had succeeded in completely losing himself amongst the beech leaves. He felt that he had no choice but to try to sneak away.

Rail was a good shot. If the target was moving slow enough and cooperated properly, then usually the said target would soon be deceased. So, the second the gun went off, Rail felt good about the shot and well he should have. In fact, the bullet was heading straight for Nethanel's heart. But it never got there. Halfway to its destination, the bullet slipped a knobby beech limb that wasn't even half an inch through. This caused the bullet's path to divert, somewhere around two one-thousandth of an inch, where it soon substantially dove into the back of a small, hard maple tree. In the end, instead of plowing into Nethanel's heart, the ill-fated bullet finally plowed deep into the heart of a seven-inch hard maple.

Nethanel took no time to celebrate. With a leap worthy of his master buck status, he disappeared from Rail's view in one massive thrust. Rail's sister-in-law's husband who had, in fact, been quite nearby when Rail's shot went off, readied his own gun just in time to witness Nethanel clear a large stone wall on the adjoining side hill by virtue, as he put it, of " ... goin' at least fifty feet in one jump!"

His grandchildren would forever be the beneficiary of this tale, usually at the end of the two or five whiskey sour or beer mark (whichever came first). Rail wished he had a good shot of something when he and his partner, looking for hair and blood, instead came upon the mortally wounded hard maple that eventually grew to a hundred feet tall and three feet through despite the deadly blow.

Nethanel, meanwhile, ran for a long time

before he slowed down. Eventually common sense prevailed, and he went to sneaking along at a good pace. He had already decided to abandon his old stomping grounds. Traveling all night in an easterly direction, he was near where he wanted to be by daybreak. He got to a place where the wind was in his favor and bedded down in some young scrub pine to rest the following day. The next evening, when it was completely black and devoid of moonlight, he rose from his bed and made his way past the knoll where he and his mother had stood when he was but a fawn. Soon thereafter he entered the territory of Crassus.

–CHAPTER 7–

Like any ordinary line buck, Nethanel took the quickest, easiest route he could find that would lead him to his ultimate destination. That destination was somewhere beyond the first line of mountains that he could see from time to time as he went along. If he had been, in fact, an ordinary line buck, then he could have been beyond that first line of foothills in three or four days. But Nethanel was no ordinary line buck.

Most line bucks, discouraged, or otherwise disillusioned, with their current breeding opportunities, would strike out in an impulsive manner for an adjoining territory or territories, depending on how aggressive they happened to feel that particular year. Once they had gotten to an area where the does were receptive, most line bucks would tend to that situation and then return to their core areas, where they had previously spent the lion's share of their lives. Nethanel had no intention of returning from whence he had come. Somewhere, up beyond those distant mountains, somewhere he would attempt, even at this late date in his life, to establish a new core area that could ultimately define what his destiny would be. He had no illusions about a new core area being handed over to him easily. This would be no quick in and out raid but an all-out campaign to actually seize control of a crucial piece of terrain.

As such then, all serious challenges to his absolute authority would have to be confronted and thoroughly defeated. Most line bucks would rely on speed and surprise to breed where it mattered and then leave as quickly as possible to avoid dangerous confrontations with the dominant resident bucks. What Nethanel was doing was so materially removed from the norm that he was assured the kind of surprise which could only be described as shock. It was very important that he take full advantage of what that shock offered him as quickly as he could.

All line bucks were looking for the best does they could, in effect, "steal" before running away. Nethanel, on the other hand, was looking for the biggest boss bucks he could find, with the intention of making them run away. Then he would own all the important does of that region during the most significant time of his life, when he was in his prime. Any offspring that he procreated at this juncture would be top shelf and bound to be a factor in the white-tail world for generations to come.

With that firmly in mind, Nethanel's rapid progress came to an abrupt end when he happened upon a large rub in the middle of an otherwise mundane flat of twenty-five-year-old poplars. Nethanel had seen this rub from a long way off. When this stand of poplars had been clear cut twenty- five years previously, one of the trees had been spared because it was too small to fool with. This was the tree which had been rubbed, and it was substantially larger than the trees around it. The stand had opened up nicely, so this larger tree stood out like a sore thumb in an otherwise undistinguished stretch of forest. Nethanel went up to it and took the measure of the beast who had made it. There was no question in Nethanel's mind as to what he had to do.

Like any good general on a campaign through hostile territory, Nethanel could not afford to leave his rear exposed to a powerful enemy force. There were other enemies up ahead. Nethanel now held the central position.

For him to ultimately achieve his objective, he must first turn and destroy one enemy before turning his attention to those living in the north. So, though the small, dark river which served as Crassus' northern border was only a night's journey away, Nethanel nevertheless chose to lay down near the big rub to rest. The warning that Crassus had intended to convey, when he had gorged the poplar, had instead transformed itself into an invitation.

Crassus had been having a fantastic fall. With his hooves propped up, figuratively speaking, on his favorite stump not far from his favorite apple orchard, he had been spending his halcyon days plucking the proverbial fattened grapes from the proverbial fattened vines. All around him, sharing his shade, the spoiled matriarchs of the surrounding countryside lounged like an obliging harem awaiting the beck and call of Crassus from his mossy couch. The sky was blue and full of nothing but the blazing benevolence of the autumn sun. Then came a small cloud from out the southeast.

Crassus had the local bucks well trained. There had been no need this season to exert himself with that obedient bunch. They knew their place and they kept to it well. But then the little cloud came, fluttering and flickering with an ever so slightly out of breath song.

The chickadee was the first of his minions to report in. At first Crassus tried to ignore her as one would a telephone call coming into the morning at an inopportune moment. But her solitary, agitated jabbering was soon followed by a host of other unwelcome voices. The party was over, and the halcyon day was ruined. It wasn't long before an unmistakable bank of dark, black clouds foretold of instability and change. The chorus coming from his many spies had a distinctly shrill note about it. Crassus reluctantly got up from his comfortable couch, angrily dispersed his bewildered harem, and then he proceeded to go to one of his nearby waiting places to see if the intruder was indeed unwise enough to show himself.

The place he chose to retire to was one of his favorites. With large rocks all around which had been deposited by the last glacier, the knoll that he headed for was a lot longer and a bit steeper than it appeared initially. The large rocks all around served to direct unsuspecting intruders directly toward a heavy line of small fir trees which guarded the crest of this knoll. Behind these fir trees were a series of slight depressions which varied greatly in depth and length. Crassus got into one as far back as he could from the top of the crest and yet still see down over it. Usually he would lay down at a time like this to conserve energy but not today. A strange and unfamiliar rage possessed him as he stood behind a young fir, searching for movement in the forest out beyond the end of the slope. He sensed that he would not have to wait long.

When the shadows grew long enough and dark enough, Nethanel rose from his daytime bed. During the day, between naps, he had succeeded in sifting through the forest hubbub, which had boiled up as a result of his presence in that region. He already knew that Crassus would not come to him.

Casually, and with a deliberation borne of complete confidence, Nethanel passed by the massive rub that Crassus had left behind. After he had torn the tree up, Crassus had carelessly set off in a straight line that would, after a couple more rubs were created, put him very near his core area. He had seen no reason to practice any guile or deception when going from rub to rub. After all, if any doe of merit should be passing by, then the rubs and scent he left around these rubs would serve as an advertisement. That was largely the reason he had been having a party when this intruder came along. And, though the scent was now faint, Nethanel had no problem following it.

For a while, Nethanel went at a steady pace, taking time to stop occasionally to do the rudimentary safety checks that traveling at night required. The birds and other animals spoke to him in their subdued way, and he was respectful of their message. Past midnight a quarter moon came up and gave him better light to go by. There didn't seem to be any imminent danger lurking anywhere, so he picked up his pace. He kept on at this speed until the faint scent he had been following suddenly came stronger to him from the forest floor.

It was when the scent from the forest floor seemed to begin coming from the air around him that Nethanel came to a halt. Seeing nothing stirring, he very carefully moved ahead for another half mile or so. He was on the edge of a narrow hardwood stand which let in light and gave him good visibility. Just beyond the hardwood was an ancient grove of hemlock. Nethanel began to feel the need to be extremely leery.

Frequently, when a resident buck detected the presence of a worthy intruder, the resident animal would usually make himself known as he came out to answer the intruder's challenge. At least that is what Nethanel had always done. Sometimes the brusqueness and the belligerent, bellicose carrying on of an obviously huge buck would be enough to cause some would-be heroes to turn tail and run away. This would always suit Nethanel just fine. A fight between equals was a serious business.

Nethanel had not heard the resident buck run away, so he knew that his host was somewhere up ahead, waiting. For the briefest of moments Nethanel was bewildered, but only for a moment. The second he recognized a hesitation arising out of that bewilderment, Nethanel instantly replaced the fear of that moment with the rage that he needed to act and to act swiftly. Whatever advantage Crassus had hoped to gain by his delaying tactic was lost, because he had delayed too long. Nethanel had regrouped and was now totally prepared to carry the initiative, no matter what game his adversary was playing.

With a purpose borne of a massive intent toward violence Nethanel crossed the narrow opening of the hardwood stand. With his powerful legs slicing like the sharpest of scissors, he sought and found a clean opening in the beginning darkness of the hemlock stand and began slipping through it toward a point of dim light on the other side of that growth. It, that point of light, drew him forward through the gloomy dampness of the ancient hemlock trees who briefly raised their mossy eyelids at the passing vitality of Nethanel's cutting gait.

It was always this way with Nethanel. Whereas others may have wondered and waited, Nethanel freely allowed the magnet of his destiny to draw him quickly, precisely, to the proper time and place that would, ultimately, reveal to him the next steps that he would have to take in the time allotted to him. The magnet was accurate this time also. After he had gone a hundred yards through the hemlock stand, a perfectly clear path beckoned to him where the hemlock ended, and a slight knoll of sparse hardwood began. As he exited the dark of the hemlock, he took a few quick mental notes as he prepared to emerge into the hardwood beyond.

The knoll didn't immediately rise from the edge of the hemlock stand. Where the forest opened up into the sparse hardwood, there was a place of flat ground before the knoll gently, slowly rose up to its fir-covered crest. There was a great jumble of rocks and boulders of varying size on either side of him, which came together toward the top of the knoll, very much like an imperfect funnel.

Heading up the hill, Nethanel saw things he liked and disliked about the rocky terrain. There were openings here and dead ends there, but he felt that he was being led into a trap that he could swing to his advantage if he read these rocks right. Sometimes getting trapped could be a good thing if both parties became subject to the same limitations. One corridor between a group of large boulders flashed into his mind, just as he caught a glimpse of low movement beyond the perimeter of juvenile fir which were strung out along the top of the knoll.

Without any preamble whatsoever, Crassus burst out from behind the thin screen of fir, lowering his oversized tine like the javelin it was, as he surged forward. It was the equivalent of a white-tail sucker punch and it almost worked. Emerging at top speed from his favorite depression hole behind the fir screen, Crassus had achieved the initial surprise, which had always served him so well in the past. He fervently sought to split Nethanel's skullcap with that lethal, downhill tine, traveling at maximum velocity. If Nethanel hadn't seen a glimpse of Crassus before the charge, then it might have been all over for him.

As it was, though, with that mighty tine roughly brushing away the dandruff from his skullcap, Nethanel managed to almost gracefully retreat toward that corridor in the rocks that he had noticed on the way up through. Applying good pressure to the right side of Crassus' rack, Nethanel deftly slipped over a nearly imperceptible, mossy rounded rock which guarded the middle of the narrow corridor. Holding off Crassus relatively easily, Nethanel carefully backed up until he felt his left rear leg and rump up against a huge, downhill boulder. Crassus, though still with an imperfect uphill advantage, was, nevertheless, for all intents and purposes, left slipping and sliding on top of the rounded rock. He was able to get his feet off to the side of the rock reasonably quickly, but, thus straddled, he couldn't really gain the leverage he needed to force the issue the way he wanted. All he could do was thrash his antlers back and forth in the unlikely hope that he could somehow deliver a lucky blow and drive his wicked tine through Nethanel's eye or some other place that mattered.

Nethanel, for his part, realized the importance of keeping the long tine neutralized. He was plenty strong enough to maintain an effective defensive position with his own massive rack to prevent any damage from that quarter, as long as he could keep his balance. Still, he wasn't after a stalemate. Now that the initial surge and surprise of Crassus's charge had dissipated, Nethanel wasn't content to let things stand pat. From experience, Nethanel knew that Crassus had expended a great deal of adrenalin and energy in that first charge. Though his rear end was secure and dug in against the boulder in back of him, Nethanel knew that the fight must be elevated to the next level. He could not just stand there and let Crassus get his second wind.

Crassus, for his part, began to perceive the futility of his current position, so he really didn't put up much of a fight when he felt Nethanel begin to slide along the surface of the big boulder which was, in effect, holding them both up. After all, was it not possible that Nethanel had seen enough and was ready to make a break for it? Stranger things had happened in the past.

However, when Nethanel finally did emerge from the rocky corridor, he showed no sign of fleeing whatsoever. Crassus jabbed his tine and twisted his rack, but Nethanel simply kept his opponent up in front of him as he was willingly pushed back down to the small flat at the base of the hill. Once he was back down on level, equal footing, then Nethanel seriously got down to the business at hand.

The flat consisted of an open area roughly twenty yards long and seven yards wide for the most part. As there was a slight drop off to soft, unstable ground heading down into the hemlock stand, from that point on, the two bucks therefore spent an inordinate amount of time trying to force each other onto that ground. Each of them understood that whoever became unbalanced first would more than likely lose the fight. Thus, the narrow flat, with its infant firs and tiny beech sap lings, became the main platform for the struggle between these equally matched animals.

The narrow spaces between their eyes flicked with the sharp edge of horn as Nethanel finally brought on his first total application of strength to see what Crassus had brought to the table. He had brought plenty. Back and forth they went, the clacking of the grinding horns growing ominously, as the antlers interwove and threatened to lock together from time to time as they struggled. Perhaps subconsciously, the fear of locking horns began to heighten their rage toward a level that they had never experienced before.

There were good reasons for equally matched bucks to avoid fighting as much as possible. Excessive expenditures of energy, due to intense fighting, over the course of the breeding season could very well leave a buck more vulnerable to the ravages of winter and to the fang of the coydog. Also, the likelihood of serious injury being sustained during a prolonged struggle between equals was high. Strained, torn muscles or broken bones did not bode well for creatures trying to survive in the wild.

But whereas depleted energy and moderate injuries could be overcome by resourceful, intelligent bucks, locked horns could not. Once these massive, virtually indestructible structures became hopelessly interlocked, it was all over for the bucks that owned them. Unfortunately, for the most part, it was always the biggest bucks, the creme of the crop, which invariably suffered this horrific fate.

Both Crassus and Nethanel instinctively knew this. Both their beautiful, magnificently crafted sets of antlers offered ample opportunity for this marriage of death. Indeed, as they sliced up the small flat with their grunting and savage pushing, they continuously worked and weaved their cruel antlers in hopes of ending the conflict as soon as possible. Those hopes were not well founded, and the longer the fight went on, the harder those antlers weaved.

Crassus had given up trying to stab or otherwise injure Nethanel with his wayward tine. Instead, he now began to craftily get the tine onto a place on Nethanel's rack where he could apply an unexpected pressure and thereby throw Nethanel into a vulnerable position, preferably onto the soft ground of the hemlock stand below. Once he got Nethanel off balance enough, got the separation he needed, then Crassus intended to put that tine right through Nethanel's neck. This fight was now a mortal one as far as Crassus was concerned.

The flat was now chewed and plowed up to the point that the ground there wasn't really any better than the soft ground of the hemlock stand. Indeed, it was so muddy and churned up, that if Rail had happened upon it the following spring, then he could have planted his potatoes in it. Both deer were beginning to wonder about this. Why worry about getting the other guy down there when it was plenty soft enough up here already? The fight was going on too long.

Nethanel began to carefully allow Crassus to have his way with the tine. He panted heavier than he really had to and let his front legs splay slightly further apart then they had been, as he apparently began to halfheartedly ward off Crassus' latest massive and violent surge.

Crassus, taking heart, wove his rack deeper and deeper into the endless morass of tines which sprouted from Nethanel's main beams. Crassus once again pretended to attempt to heave Nethanel toward the hemlock mud. His massive tine now lay across the main beam of Nethanel's left side antler and had succeeded in tying into the base of Nethanel's G-2 tine. Crassus twisted around with his own left side antler, until he felt Nethanel's center of balance shift to counter the force of that twisting. Just as Crassus was preparing to press down with the tine, Nethanel, in a superb feat of physical agility and strength, gathered himself tightly together, and, before Crassus could fully react, he suddenly lifted with all the strength that his powerful neck could muster.

Crassus had been using all his energy and guile in a move to throw Nethanel to the uphill side of the small flat. However, when Nethanel successfully completed his movement, the front legs of Crassus began to leave the ground. Before they became completely airborne, there came a surprisingly loud crack, similar to a gunshot. The great tine of Crassus had snapped off and was hurled ignominiously onto the uphill side of the knoll, while Crassus himself flew down into the mud of the hemlock swamp.

Though he had been momentarily stunned by the force created by the breaking tine, Crassus didn't waste any time wondering what had happened. With a speed borne of desperation and the need to survive, he got to his feet before Nethanel, who had himself been thrown off balance by the snapping of the tine, and was ready to begin the pursuit. The fight was over.

Crassus knew that Nethanel would be out for blood now. He sensed, rather than saw, Nethanel bringing his rack down the hill to gouge and gore. It was only by pure luck that his hind legs found a sturdy hemlock root to push off from when he began his desperate attempt to escape. After he completed his first successful leap, Crassus also had the good fortune to land on a reasonably solid patch of sturdy moss for his second leap.

Nethanel, seeing nothing but red, started to

give pursuit but, on his first leap, hit nothing but soft, gooey mud. Instantly, he was at it again but when he saw Crassus fly away on the second leap, Nethanel simply took to watching the departure for a few seconds. If Crassus had even given the appearance of stopping, then Nethanel would have pursued him until one of their hearts gave out. But he now knew that Crassus would keep going, and not for just a short distance either.

Nethanel was right. Crassus fled wildly at first. When he realized that he wasn't being pursued, he slowed down but kept moving in a disconsolate manner. Eventually, he crossed over into a quiet corner of a territory that Nethanel had only recently abandoned. There he lived on in an unpretentious fashion, but he was never the same again.

Nethanel, after the departure of Crassus, rubbed a tree or two in vexation before seriously testing the wind. To the north, not far away, lay the apple orchard which Crassus had loved so much. The matriarchs there shifted languidly and calmly awaited the new lord of the house.

–CHAPTER 8–

Athaliah had been resting. The grey appearing on her muzzle told of her need, of her right to regain some of the energy she and her pack had expended, hunting the night before. It had been a futile hunt so at the end of it, just before dawn was breaking, she had led her family of seven to the perimeter of a different hunting ground.

Two of the seven were this year's pups who had survived from the spring litter and were more of a liability than anything else. Still, they were learning, and, helped along mightily by her eldest son, Zadoc, they were now doing their part in jumping and turning game. All they needed was a little more time and a lot more food. If anyone could provide that for them it was Athaliah.

She had assumed the position of matriarch of this group six years ago. She was old for a coydog and if there was anything which passed for wisdom among her kind, she possessed it. She had learned through hard experience where to go and when to do it. Sometimes the numbers of her pack grew quite cumbersome, but, for the time being, the amount of hungry mouths that she was responsible for was manageable. She knew where the game flowed, and she had become adept at casting her net.

But this year had been challenging. A cold, wet spring had seriously depleted an already fragile grouse population. It, the cold weather, hadn't helped the turkey flock either, but turkeys were difficult to hunt even in the best of times. The squirrels were still around, noisy as ever, but the voles had pretty much headed for their winter beds. Rabbits never did rebound from their low point, which had occurred when Athaliah's kind had first arrived here some four decades ago. Grubs, insects and songbirds were okay in a pinch but more was needed. That's when Athaliah remembered the old apple orchard which lay just ahead of them down the valley.

It had been a great consolation to her when she had thought of that orchard. Surely there would be grouse, rabbits and deer there! If they could avoid the shin-fa who would probably be lurking there hunting deer, then perhaps the pack could actually benefit from the malignant behavior of the shin-fa. There could be one or more gut piles there or, better yet, a wounded deer who had been savagely touched by the terrible black horn of the shin-fa. Who could say, there might even be the sumptuous gut pile of a bear or a wounded bear taking its last breath. The possibilities were suddenly endless.

First though, there was the need to rest. Though the initial hints of hunger pains were making themselves known, the need for a beneficial rest had to be answered. However, as is often the case, the rest for the weary could never be guaranteed. For, just as Athaliah was beginning to embrace the first of her dreams that morning, a faint, familiar noise came gently to her on the prevailing breeze and rudely sidled up beside her hunger pains. She tried to ignore the sound at first, because she was very tired, but when it came to her more forcefully on a slightly harder wind, she had no choice but to open her eyes. It was the sound of deer antlers clashing somewhere in the direction they were intending to go. She tried to gauge the intensity of the conflict, but it was so far away that she had to be satisfied with knowing what it was. Fighting deer were sometimes hurt deer. So, as tired as she was, she had no choice but to rouse her reluctant crew to press on down the valley as quickly, and as carefully, as they could.

Nethanel wasted no time getting to Crassus' harem. He didn't want to alarm them, but he also didn't want to give another big buck the chance to move in now that Crassus was out of the picture. Nethanel hadn't been hurt in the fighting, but he certainly had stretched his muscles as much as he wanted to in that fashion for one day. A softer, gentler exertion might be okay though . . . With that in mind, he began to cast about for the harem's exact location.

This had proved to be a bit more difficult than Nethanel had first imagined. Crassus didn't like to upset his ladies so, as much as possible, whenever his minions had reported that an intruder was about, he would leave the important does at a comfortable place while he went off to do battle. The harem wasn't that far off from where he and Nethanel had met, but just before Crassus had left the group, he had given them an ominous roll of his fearsome rack to help them understand that their chastity and fidelity were not optional. Particularly not for the two leading matriarchs that he had been entertaining for the past several years. The extended family could do what they wanted, but the matriarchs were his.

As they obeyed Crassus' wishes to the letter, Nethanel consequently had to roam around more then he ordinarily would have imagined. Ultimately, however, it wasn't all that long before the twitch of an ear and the appearance of a wide eye of surprise gave their location away. They were laying down on the far northern edge of the apple orchard. The does knew what was going on, but they wisely stayed put to let Nethanel present himself in the manner which he saw fit. After all, it wouldn't do to get too cozy right away. For all they knew Crassus could show up at any second.

All and all, though, things were soon going outstandingly well, when there came an abrupt bark of alarm from a member of the extended family, who had been on guard far down the hill. That was the direction of the danger, so Nethanel instinctively got himself hidden behind the matriarchs. He wouldn't leave them willingly, but he had to make sure he knew what he was facing if the alarm turned out not to be false. It wasn't.

Fortunately for him the matriarchs were not in full heat yet. They were well on their way, but they weren't there entirely. Now he could use them for cover before breaking away from them if he had to. That would have been difficult, if not impossible, to do if their estrus cycle had been at a crucial stage.

Initially, Nethanel had hoped that the current disturbance was caused by a forlorn, solitary shin-fa heading back home for dinner. However, far off a flicker of movement, hungry and earnest, promptly set his antlers into motion as he proceeded to put the does around him into a swift response. The does weren't happy about this turn of events, but they immediately obeyed nevertheless, because it was evident that Nethanel meant business. Besides, they instinctively knew that their future success depended on keeping this master buck alive.

The younger, less important does of the extended family rushed by first. After they had run at full speed for a short distance, they slowed down and let first Nethanel, and then the two matriarchs, go past them into the thick brush of a ravine below the apple orchard. There was no need for abject flight yet. It was obvious that they were the object of the coydogs' attention, but it was still unclear how much energy their chief enemy was going to expend on what the deer knew would be a foolhardy effort. There was no deep, crusty snow, the weather was fine, and their would-be prey was almost absurdly healthy. Still, the coydogs were obviously hungry and if any of the deer made a stupid mistake or showed any sign of weakness or illness, then the pursuit by the coydogs would be relentless, remorseless, and, in all probability, effective to a lethal degree.

Nethanel had lived long enough to understand that this particular group of coydogs were introducing themselves to him. That was yet another problem with fighting. Besides everything else that could go wrong, it, the fighting, would usually draw attention to one's self. It might, as it was in this case, it might come from the coydogs, it might come from the shin-fa, it might come sooner, and it might come later, but no matter how or when it came, breaking the silence of the forest, by smashing against another massive buck, was always a sure way to allow a lot of nasty things to come into an already precarious existence.

These coydogs were checking him out to see if he was hurt. He knew that he wasn't, but he also knew that he had to be rid of these predators as soon as possible. Running around at breakneck speed for a protracted period of time, at this time of the year, was highly inadvisable.

His mother had taught him not to do it, or, if he had to do it, then to do it as little as possible. That bark from the subordinate doe a few minutes ago, to warn of impending danger, could have been brought on by the presence of a shin-fa. Running in wild panic when the shin-fa were about was the quickest way to get killed that he could think of. Still, the thought of the long fangs of two or three powerful coydogs ripping apart his hind legs was more than enough to keep him weaving about, as the deer blasted out of the ravine and surged along the edge of a long, narrow bog.

Nethanel knew what he was looking for. Though very tired, he was not afraid. He easily kept up with the herd in front of him. He bounced along, letting his great white flag blend in with the others as they fled. Pretty soon, with the young softwood in the area helping with a camouflaging effect, pretty soon all the pursuing coydogs could make out was a bewildering mosaic of white patches moving unevenly away from them in an unpredictable manner.

As far as running along with wild abandon, the coydogs were on a timetable also. Yes, they were hungry, but were not the shin-fa about? Several times Athaliah had heard the sudden thunder on sunny days that would reduce her family by one. This type of pursuit was best reserved for cold, rainy days when the shin-fa were in their dens. But had she not heard the antlers rattling? Was it not worth the gamble to test the worthiness of the buck in front of them? If he were old or weak, then he would provide food for the entire pack for several days. They would devour his meat, his guts, the marrow of his bones, and even his fat laden hide. These were the thoughts of Athaliah as she led her crew after the fleeing deer. The attempt had to be made.

Still, it wasn't long before she recognized the telltale signs of an organized series of evasive steps that the deer were taking. There was no doubt in her mind that contact with the deer could be maintained indefinitely, but was it worth it? They were hungry, not crazy. If a worthwhile subject of the hunt could not be singled out very soon, then the hunt would have to be called off.

Athaliah slowed her headlong pursuit, and when she had safely entered a nearly impenetrable clump of thick young fir, she held up. Soon all the other members of the pack were hovering about, seeking instruction and reassurance. She wasn't ready to give up just yet. The one that drew her here, the buck, had to be tested further. She knew how the bucks worked. She gave her orders. Keeping the younger members close to her, she would press ahead to keep the deer herd boiling and moving for a while longer. She then sent Zadoc, her oldest and most reliable son, off to the side to make a large circle around their current position. It would be up to him to determine where the buck had broken off from the herd and to, if possible, see whether or not he merited any further attention.

Athaliah did not recognize Nethanel's track. As this was a part of her territory, it had become her business over the years to know which bucks had lived long enough to become the dominant animals in any given region. A big buck had tracks which, through wear and tear, were specific to them. She had known the tracks of Crassus, particularly his left hind track. She wished she were trailing Crassus now, because this newcomer had apparently displaced him. He, Crassus, might not be in any shape nor mood to run like this deer was. Still, there was always room for hope. This new deer, being unfamiliar with the terrain, might not be quite so inclined to go very far from the matriarchs. Athaliah pressed on, confident that if anyone could locate the newcomer it would be Zadoc.

Nethanel had in fact broken off from the other deer. After they had gone a long way down the side of the bog, a berm had developed, which had roughly broken the bog into two distinct halves. The berm was uniformly covered with young pine and hemlock. The two matriarchs, who were intimately familiar with the territory, took a right when they got to the crest of the berm. The direction they were headed was the obvious way to go. Beyond the berm the narrow bog which they had been traveling along broke open into a larger bog, which was obviously on its way to turning into a substantial swamp. All the deer kept to the right in a speedy, yet orderly, fashion, following the abundant cover on their way toward the big swamp beyond. All the deer except Nethanel, that is.

Athaliah had been right to test him. Though the chase had not been going on that long, Nethanel had already had enough of it. Crassus had been a worthy opponent, and all this extracurricular activity was beginning to get to Nethanel. He needed to remove himself from the chase as soon as possible, before he overexerted himself. Deer can only run at full speed for so long, and, under the circumstances, Nethanel had reached his limit.

Sensing a slight pause behind him, Nethanel got the two matriarchs to slow down momentarily so he could get to the front of them and the other deer. He then headed down the clearest path until he saw what he wanted. To his left, fifteen feet from where he was now traveling, were two medium-sized, bushy fir trees whose bottom limbs, in their search for the sun, had grown long and very low to the ground. They covered the ground completely.

Nethanel found a flat, stable rock of sufficient size and proceeded to use it to launch himself in a superbly delicate manner toward those bottom fir branches. With nary a sound, he landed in the midst of these covering needles, and then he calmly snuck between the two firs. He went a few feet more and then he waited.

Once they saw that Nethanel was positioned, then the matriarchs sprang into action. They, along with some of the youngsters, carefully eased past the flat rock that Nethanel had launched from, and then they broke into a dead run, letting a flag or two flip into the air as they did so. They chopped up the ground more than they had to in passing. One of the matriarchs even intentionally proceeded to slosh through a leaf strewn mud flat and made quite a mess of it. Now, from the point where Nethanel had leapt toward the fir trees, it was very easy to look down the path where most of the deer had gone and see where a large deer had fled in obvious panic. A coydog on the hunt would not be able to resist these signs of a panicked confusion.

But Nethanel was not panicked. Staying to the bottom of the berm, on the side facing the large swamp, he did the unexpected and did it well. Once the berm left the bog, it flattened out and became a low ridge rising up through a stand of hardwood trees. Picking his spots and staying low, he gradually, but steadily, made his way up this low slope. Every once in a while, he would halt behind a large rock or a small, leafy beech tree to smell the air ahead of him and to check for movement off his left side or below him. Trusting the diligence of the two worthy matriarchs, he was now more concerned with the possible presence of shin-fa then he was the coydogs. He felt that if they were still after him in earnest, then he would have seen or heard of some evidence that his ruse down in the bog had been sniffed out.

However, for the time being, Nethanel deemed it advisable to get further up the hill to where there was a definable height of the land. There he would rest. He went another quarter mile until the rounded berm knoll essentially disappeared as it merged with a much steeper ridge. Nethanel went left up along this ridge, because he could make out the tops of some large oak trees not too far up the hill.

All was quiet when he finally got up to them, and he was rewarded for his effort with a handful of large acorns. After taking time to eat a few, he then went up past the oak stand. He would save the majority of the bitter nuts for later on. There was a band of low hemlock not too far up ahead of him which had caught his attention. When he got up to these trees, he was satisfied with what he saw. There was a weak sun breaking through some persistent November clouds and what heat there was in that sun seemed to be settling right in here. With the hemlock gathering around him to protect him from being seen from behind, Nethanel proceeded to get a low flat rock, about the same size as his body, in front of him. From this vantage point he could accurately keep track of what was transpiring far down the hill. It wasn't perfect but it would do for now. It had been a hard day, so it wasn't long after he had rested his head on his knees that Nethanel was sleeping the fitful sleep of the hunted.

Zadoc had done his duty. Roaming near, then far, he had been weaving a large, very uneven circle. He had ceased his hunting lope often in hopes of hearing the urgent cry of the pack, telling him that they badly needed his help in taking down a victim. However, as time went on, he stopped less and less as it became painfully evident that the hunt had not been successful. Still, the deer that they had been primarily chasing was a big one, so Zadoc had made his circle as wide as he dared to without potentially letting the buck double back around to safety.

But there was a timetable for such things. Wasting energy on a wild goose chase was never encouraged. That was a good way to curtail an already short life span. So, after he had done the best he could to find the "injured" buck, he consequently began to seek out the quickest, easiest path back downhill to find the pack.

At the crest of a sharp ridge he stopped and stood for one more time to look and listen for something encouraging. When nothing was forthcoming, Zadoc gave up entirely and pitched carelessly down the slope toward the bog. Going at a good clip, he went around a thick clump of mountain hemlock and caught a shimmer of movement behind him. It was the buck that he was supposed to be helping to corral. Zadoc's head stopped and his body came around to face the massive animal in front of him. At first, of course, there was an initial surge of triumph and the hope of a future dinner. That was a very fleeting interpretation of what was actually transpiring, however.

The buck was only twenty-five feet away and he was regarding Zadoc very coldly. In fact, after only a few scant seconds, Zadoc realized that he was well within the dangerous wheelhouse of an extremely grumpy, testosterone-laden deer. The buck's antlers were by far the biggest that Zadoc had ever seen, and they were perched on a body whose huge size deemed them almost to the point of being insignificant. Zadoc was a fairly large coydog, but the creature in front of him was six or seven times his weight, and the antlers were beginning to shift position.

As the buck's horns slowly assumed an aggressive posture, some of the great, sharp blades within the rack began to reflect the weak rays of the autumn sun. In some of those vicious blades, Zadoc could almost see himself reflected as with an imperfect mirror similar to the ones medieval folks used to gaze into when those folks were contemplating their own mortality. Zadoc's illusion of feasting and resting evaporated instantly. He was in his prime and capable of great bursts of speed when the occasion called for it. The occasion was screaming at him right now. Relying on nothing but raw, pure instinct, he managed to get the jump on Nethanel. For a long, brief moment, Zadoc was aware of a great angry mass close behind him. He made it into some low beeches, and the danger was soon past, though you never would have known it by the way Zadoc was streaking down the hill.

Because of his youth and his unbelievable athletic ability, he soon realized that he had made it. But Zadoc was surly and short-tempered when he came upon his pack milling around aimlessly in the swamp. He even snapped at the young ones who came crowding around him hoping for good news. This caused Athaliah to come up to his muzzle, demanding an explanation for his rude behavior. He quickly submitted and then gave her the rundown.

"Yeah, yeah, I found him. He's plenty healthy all right, that's why I didn't call out. He'll outlive us all."

Athaliah, pragmatic as always, snapped roughly at the rambunctious youngsters who had been a pain in the butt all day, running happily ahead of everyone else and threatening to ruin what could have been a productive hunt if the big buck had cooperated. Anyway, now it was back to the apple orchard to spend the rest of the day scrounging for squirrels and grubs.

Nethanel had given it his best shot; he had never killed a coydog before, but if that one had stumbled, then he would have tried. It had been a rough day, and he hadn't appreciated being woken up out of a sound sleep. Luckily the coydog had been alone. If the pack had been around, then the story may have had a different ending. That, probably more than anything else, was the reason Nethanel had chased the young coydog with such venom. He had been caught with his pants down and it had scared him a bit.

However, his fear and anger had quickly dissipated almost as rapidly as that coydog had disappeared. No reason to waste energy nor to be foolish. That pack was still down there somewhere, and he intended to go in the opposite direction. The short time of rest was over.

He made his way back up the hill to the oak stand he had gone past earlier. He was intending to save the acorns there for later that evening, but the plan had changed. In an orderly and effective manner, he found and ate the biggest acorns that were available there. Then carefully, but without stopping, he set off in a long arc that would bring him toward the opposite side of the large swamp that the rest of the deer had disappeared into earlier that day. On a steep hill overlooking the swamp, he laid down to wait for night. Soon he would rejoin the matriarchs. Hopefully all the excitement of the day had promoted a significant advance toward estrus, otherwise the horns would have to come into play one more time that day. He was all done being mister nice guy. He had a long way to go and not much time to get there.

–CHAPTER 9–
Sertorius

Felix had noticed something. Whenever a different or important thing came into the immediate vicinity, the big deer, Sertorius, would rotate his left ear. His other ear, injured in some long-ago fight, could only come about halfway up and so was barely used at all. His right eye also bore evidence of the old trauma, though apparently it still functioned properly. It must have been a tremendous battle, for Sertorius was a huge deer who held his giant, open woods' rack easily and with a good deal of grace and majesty.

The rack aside, however, it was the left ear that Felix had mostly concentrated on when he had first met Sertorius some three years before. At that time, he was scarcely more than a weanling and on his own. Just before the time of that meeting Felix had watched his mother and sister get torn apart and devoured by the resident coydogs.

Using what rudimentary lessons his mother had managed to impart to him at that vulnerable age, Felix had escaped from that horrific scene duly impressed. Frightened, lonely and heading he knew not where, he had wandered aimlessly for quite some time. He really wasn't ready to be totally alone yet. Without trying that hard, he eventually covered quite a bit of ground.

His main objective was to keep as far away from the coydogs as he could. He wasn't able to accomplish that without becoming hopelessly lost. As he was very young, he hadn't accumulated any familiarity with the countryside at large. His time in this world was becoming increasingly uncertain with each passing day. But if the days were harsh, then the nights were even worse. In the pitch black of night, the great horned owls seemed to be perpetually perched over him, and the coydogs apparently ran laps around him just for the enjoyment of tormenting him before they got around to tearing him to pieces.

Finally, one day after yet another fearful night, finally a group of large dark clouds gathered on a nearby horizon and started grumbling amongst themselves. Felix decided it was time to head for higher ground to escape the deluge that was apparently the next misery that he would have to endure. Big fat drops of cold rain were starting to fall when he crawled beneath the kind of low, heavy spruce that his mother had taught him to use when he was caught out in the rain away from the den.

He was just settling in against the base of a spruce when he glanced over and froze. There, not six feet away, was a massive white-tail buck snuggled up against the neighboring tree. The buck, Sertorius, was regarding Felix with a look which contained a mixture of curiosity and, well, amusement. Sertorius found the fox pup interesting. He also sensed that the fox was vulnerable and frightened.

Foxes seldom made any trouble, unless a deer was severely injured or otherwise showing signs of an extreme sort of infirmity. Even then, when a deer was very low and close to death, even then, a mature and experienced fox would not choose to rush the process any. In most cases under these circumstances, foxes were scavengers, not hunters. Sertorius could see that this young fox poised no danger to himself. Instead, Sertorius chose to tolerate Felix and actually took some comfort in the young animal's closeness.

Felix came to understand that the big deer was going to permit his presence, as long as he kept still and minded his own business. And it didn't take very long for the fox to reap the benefit of being so near to such an experienced and even-tempered buck. It rained hard that afternoon and even after the thunder and lightning had stopped, Sertorius remained in his bed. Felix was just growing restless, when he noticed the left ear of Sertorius coming to attention and swiveling to catch some sound coming up the hill. The deer's demeanor changed, also, as the universal language of concern, if not actual fear, soon drew its icy cloak over the deer's body posture. Felix, who had been quiet and motionless while all this was transpiring, remained still and in place even as the great deer calmly rose from his bed and prepared to leave the sanctuary of the spruce.

Felix didn't know what was up, but he nevertheless did not hesitate to emulate his new benefactor's retreat. In doing so, he was very careful not to move too suddenly or do anything else that might draw attention to either himself or Sertorius. Once out in the open, the young fox, being much smaller than the deer, was able to utilize an entirely different route of escape than the deer was using. The retreat was successfully completed without Felix being either a bother or a liability. This time it had been the deer who had warned the fox. In the future this role was freely reversed back and forth, depending on who saw the danger first. To ingratiate himself to Sertorius, whom Felix viewed as being a great benefactor after this first episode, the little fox would frequently allow himself to be seen by their pursuers, while escaping, and thereby distract potential enemies, while Sertorius got cleanly away. In this way a bond of mutual trust was soon developed.

As the bond grew stronger over time, Felix and Sertorius enlarged and perfected their unusual friendship. The majority of their time, especially during the rut, was spent apart, though the young fox liked to keep tabs on his big friend, as much as possible. The differing needs of their respective species, however, required a lot of adaptation on the part of the fox. By and large, foxes liked to hunt by day. Sertorius, being the dominant buck of this region, was mostly resting and otherwise laying low during the day when the rut was on. So, whenever the deer bedded down for the day the fox either took off or was very careful not to move around too much if he was in Sertorius' vicinity. Felix was smart enough to stay out of the way and yet keep an eye out for potential danger at the same time.

It wasn't long before Felix developed some habits that the deer found very useful indeed. Depending what the intrusion was, the fox usually had two means of dealing with it. If the danger came from an approaching shin-fa, Felix would give either one or two quick barks. If the shin-fa was sneaking in from the left, then Felix would let out one yip. If the opposite was true, then the clever little fox would give up two subdued yet very audible barks. Generally speaking, if the shin-fa was a hunter then Sertorius would more than likely already be fully aware of the human's approach. One time, however, the barks from the alert fox woke Sertorius from a deeper slumber than he had intended to be in. Obviously, it only took one time to matter.

If the intrusion was anything other than a shin-fa, then the fox would not risk barking. Instead, Felix would run past where Sertorius was sleeping and make sure that the buck was awake when he did so. If necessary, Felix would actually stop and make a small ruckus if Sertorius was dreaming deeply about the previous night's gallantries.

If Felix crossed from the left, then that's where Sertorius would focus his attention, and vice-versa. Felix would not do this unless he felt that the buck absolutely needed to know that something was up. The fox had different ways of carrying himself, and his body language would convey the presence of either one of two things: the coming of coydogs or the coming of another dangerous, massive buck.

Sertorius didn't have a lot of these white-tail intruders, for the would-be interlopers of that region had been thoroughly educated. Sertorius was a ''compression'' buck. Between the end of the coastal plain and the beginning of the real mountains of western Maine and northern New Hampshire lay a band of exaggerated foothills. It wasn't a huge area, but it was an important one, because it was here that the genetic pools of north and south were squeezed together like grease lubricating a ball bearing. Sertorius was the latest force controlling the flow of this grease.

At just under three hundred pounds, Sertorius was the very picture of athleticism. His body was so long that he almost appeared to be slender at first glance. For the shin-fa, the first glance was usually all they ever saw of Sertorius, for his intelligence far exceeded his impressive physical stature. Using the ground of the foothills to full advantage, ducking behind the crests of the exaggerated ravines, that he knew in intimate detail, before skirting along or into the edges of the big swamps, which always intruded where the foothills weren't, Sertorius, even when there was snow on the ground, Sertorius always mystified and avoided even the most diligent hunters, be they man or beast.

Deer are naturally powerful animals, but, like any athlete, steady and persistent exercise will significantly sharpen what nature provides. For Sertorius, his intelligence and his athletic prowess went hand and hand. His intelligence made him curious. As a youngster, his mother had rigorously impressed upon him the need to know every aspect of his immediate surroundings. In the short time he had spent with her, she became deeply content that the base she had provided for him would serve him well. All his life Sertorius would endlessly go up and down the foothills he lived in, in an almost neurotic manner. This provided him with an intimate knowledge of every crook and cranny of every hill and swamp for miles around. It also made him very strong. He was what the shin-fa called a "ridge runner."

Of course, it didn't do any good to be very strong in one didn't have the hardware to back that strength up. Sertorius had the hardware. Most of the big bucks in his area had the classic rack of the swamp deer. These racks came up over the top of the buck's head, and, though they could be massive in length and girth, they were generally narrow, relatively speaking. These racks had developed this way through the ages to allow the deer that wore them easier passage through the thick brush of the many swamps which more or less surrounded the entire area of the first foothills.

The rack of Sertorius was of the mountains to the north. Borne of eons of grazing through the open oak groves which had grown up after the last ice age, these racks, besides being of admirable length and girth, were also capable of promoting a magnificent width. The inside width of Sertorius' rack was just over thirty inches. His G-2 tines exceeded thirteen inches. On some deer this rack could have appeared ostentatious, but on Sertorius it all came off as understated. By anybody's definition Sertorius was a beautiful deer.

Beautiful, that is, as long as you didn't intend to oust him from his hood. If that were the case, if you were a big bad buck coming to shake down the master, then you would be the beholder of a beauty which could only be perceived as a bleak and austere thing. Yes, if you were there to take over what Sertorius considered to be his, then you were bound to take the full measure of his most visible attributes. For, besides being an aesthetically pleasing enticement for the does of his region, Sertorius also used his rack perfectly when it came time for him to intimidate and conquer his opponents. Many a carpetbagger was escorted roughly from the castle of Sertorius at the end of a speedy and ill-natured tine.

Sertorius couldn't always dictate where he would fight his foes, but if he could use his ceaseless rambling and encyclopedic knowledge of his home range to his full advantage then, of course, he would. A bare, slippery ledge here, a tangled tricky bunch of ground hemlock there, and pretty soon you had another would-be hero scrambling for the quickest exit away from Sertorius that he could find. Knowing where the soft spots were and what the uphill sections looked like above those soft spots, always held a macabre sort of fascination for Sertorius. At the very least, getting above any adversary so that he, Sertorius, would appear to be around ten feet tall, was always the first order of business when it came time for combat.

Fighting around cliffs or along the sharp crests of steep ravines always filled Sertorius with a certain, grim delight. He never once shied away from going head to head with any massive buck on level ground, but if there was some way he could utilize his intimate knowledge of his home territory, then he would certainly endeavor to do so. Sertorius had no qualms whatsoever about enticing a foolish foe into making an ill-conceived charge, which would usually end up compromising that foe's life and limb.

Slick damp ledges, old ground hemlock, uneven terrain hidden by thick masses of stunted pine or beech saplings were the staple diet of misadventures handed out by this big, sinewy buck as he successfully defended his home range from all comers year after year. Sertorius consequently became supremely confident of his abilities, and rightly so.

And, although the pseudonym of "ridge runner" fit him aptly, he was, in fact, more than that. Sertorius was a student of his environment, and his size and physical prowess constituted only part of his success. More importantly then all that he was, far and away, the most intelligent buck of the "compression" district. He had the ability to create plans quickly and to execute those plans with a brilliant dispatch. From his north and from his south they came. If they were lucky they left much quicker then they arrived.

Several of them stayed forever, for Sertorius was merciless when he gained an advantage. It didn't take long for most of his opponents to realize the full gravity of the situation that they were in when Sertorius made his presence known.

Over the years word got around. In a tough neighborhood, Sertorius was known as a tough customer, a customer best left alone. This particular year had been very peaceful, and there was no real reason to believe that this peaceful condition would be in any way disturbed. But these things, these periods of calm and conflict, had always seemed to come in waves which eventually evolved into a partially predictable and therefore manageable condition of day to day living. One had only to face up to the fact that when you were at the top of the heap, then eventually there was going to be a hassle.

But Sertorius was in the prime of his life, and therefore he wasn't particularly concerned about confronting hassles. The inevitable result of every fight that he had been in over the past few years had served to completely reinforce an unflagging conviction that he had been right, right to do whatever it was that he had done before, during, and after those fights. Watching the rapidly disappearing rear end of yet another vanquished foe showed him this—showed him that he had been right, right to choose the ground that he had selected which had, in turn, enabled him to use the right tactics, which had so unnerved and otherwise unraveled his supposedly worthy opponents. And, if a foolish intruder persisted, refused to accept the inevitable, then Sertorius would not hesitate to go right to the ground with him and, invariably, drive one of his wickedly long G-2 tines right through that pretender's foolish neck or some other vital area.

His propensity for extreme violence was a well-known commodity within the local white-tail community for some time now. It was perhaps because of this that Sertorius had been enjoying a peaceful breeding season this year. But in the back of his mind Sertorius knew that this was a false peace, a false calm. Something in the air at the end of summer had unsettled him. That feeling of unease had never really left him during this period of unusual calm. He had felt this way before, as with the calm felt during the bluebird day ahead of a big storm. He had no way of knowing that there was actually trouble coming, so he was beginning to entertain the disturbing possibility that he had been wrong about something. The very notion that he had somehow been mistaken about feeling this unease, had lately been more upsetting to him than any robust challenger that the surrounding mountains could have conjured up.

But one had to be practical about such things. Any unnecessary fretting or useless squandering of energy or time, which should be used for rest and the consolidation of finite life forces, was a weakness which Sertorius had never allowed to develop before. But now this weakness, this unease, was fast becoming unchecked in nature. Sertorius was all about being right, and he was having a real difficulty with being wrong.

Felix had long sensed a kind of peevishness in his big friend's mannerisms and didn't know what to make of it. For long days he kept off to one side and went on long sojourns to help locate the probable source of the buck's discomposure. It was getting a little worse all the time, so finally on a sunny, quiet day, Felix just plain gave up and settled down to rest with Sertorius on one of the buck's' favorite ledges overlooking a large brook. He, Felix, was about to go to sleep in the warm afternoon sun when, almost to his relief, he saw the left ear of Sertorius flicker with agitation and alarm.

–CHAPTER 10–

Nethanel moved at a steady pace. He didn't hurry, for he was in no rush, but he did move at a speed which, while keeping him safe, was nevertheless succeeding in putting large hunks of territory behind him in a surprisingly short period of time. Occasionally as he went along, he would seek out a high spot where he could look out toward the north. He felt that he knew exactly where he was going.

Gradually the mountains he was seeking, once only hazy apparitions bequeathed to him by the ghost of his mother, gradually the mountains he needed to be in began to come sharply into focus. The clearer they became, the more he converted into a true line buck, a buck who would travel day and night despite all hardships and danger until his goal had been achieved. Other than death, it would be all but impossible for anything to divert him from his mission. Unless, of course, unless it was a force which, like death, could not be readily, or wisely, ignored.

It happened while he was hurtling along just below the crest of a sharp ridge topped off with young pine. He was watching his step along the uneven slope of the hillside, when something he saw out of the corner of his eye caused him to veer uphill to a level spot where he could completely swing around and stop. He couldn't believe his eyes.

There, across a narrow, dark ravine, placed in an obviously ostentatious manner, was a cedar tree seven inches in diameter, which was freshly rubbed to warn all potential intruders to move out of this particular area. Nethanel's world was instantly transformed into the red of an unreasonable rage. This rage had to have an outlet immediately. Nearby on the ridge he was standing on, Nethanel spotted an eight-inch pine tree that was directly opposite from the cedar tree across the way. Savagely he attacked the pine with the intention of busting it apart. When it became apparent that that was not going to happen, Nethanel gouged and gored the helpless pine with an unreasonable viciousness before scraping the ground around it and then applying a liberal amount of urine to the torn earth for good measure.

He had neither expected nor wanted this turn of events. Crassus had been a formidable foe. For another buck of equal or even greater magnitude to be living so close to that vanquished master buck was an astonishing reality that Nethanel was not prepared for. But this was a compression area, and, as time went on, Nethanel would simply have to adjust to the fact that important deer would always be arriving, and disappearing, with an alarming regularity here. If he was to survive, he would simply have to be equal to the task of maintaining a grip on the places that would matter.

For a brief moment he stood there, breathing heavily, as he stared into his handiwork on the young pine. Before too long the rut would be getting late. Momentarily, Nethanel considered moving on toward his northern goal. Did he not have an adequate message prepared for this resident bumpkin? Would he not see the imminent danger and promptly move away in an obliging manner? Could not this pretender find a permanent satisfaction by accepting an easy and safe exile to the furthest most limits of his territory? Well no . . . no, no, no, no, no. Nethanel knew full well the answer was no. This buck was going nowhere voluntarily.

The matriarchs who had belonged to Crassus were now a fixture in Nethanel's future. They mattered, and they mattered a lot. If his plans worked out as he envisioned them, then every year for the rest of his productive breeding life, he would have to journey down here to place his stamp on their future. With Crassus gone, some other buck might get the wild idea that those does should belong to him and not Nethanel. This local yokel who had seen fit to tear the bark off a seven-inch cedar tree was obviously such a buck. He would take the generosity of Nethanel removing the mighty Crassus to the fullest extent possible, and the reality of this profane abuse of good manners filled Nethanel anew with a blinding rage.

Carelessly, he surged down into the dark ravine with the intent of violating the immediate area surrounding the cedar rub. Urinating, scraping the ground, busting up small trees, and spearing the offending cedar, Nethanel prepared himself for what he knew was coming. In the world of white-tail etiquette, he was being a real bastard and he didn't even care. It didn't really matter whether or not the buck responsible for the cedar rub bore witness to the various sacrileges that Nethanel had just committed. That buck obviously held sway over a large hunk of the white-tail world in these parts. Nethanel was now telling everybody that the gig was up. He was the new sheriff in town, in his own mind at least. Translating that theory into fact would be his next objective.

The afternoon sun was already translating through the silent forest. This was a dangerous time of the day for a big buck to be slicing recklessly around in the woods. The shin-fa were about. He had smelt them, and though they weren't close, as far as he could tell, they were nevertheless near enough to give him pause. He had been moving most of the night before and all that day. Before he went any further, Nethanel realized that he needed something to eat and a sensible period of rest.

In the way that all deer of his stature have, he pretty well knew the direction that he would have to travel the next morning and roughly how far he would probably have to go. The way the tree had been rubbed, the way it had been scented, and the way the buck had carelessly, openly, left the area told Nethanel a lot of what he needed to know. This guy didn't seem to have a care in the world. Briefly, Nethanel's vision turned to its unfriendly, rosy hue before he regained control of himself.

He lifted his nose to catch the telltale scent of some oak which were growing along the outside perimeter of the softwood patch that he was now standing in. Various creatures had been feeding under a select few of these oaks and had either eaten their fill or had been frightened off while they were in the act of eating. The half-eaten or partially cracked open acorns left by the animals emitted a slight odor which Nethanel was quick to pick up on and follow.

However, though Nethanel soon found the food he needed, he was nevertheless not happy. He had been in deep, line-buck mode, which was intended to evaporate a considerable distance that he felt he needed to travel to achieve a foggy goal that he hoped he would understand only once he got to the place of anointment. But Nethanel had already disregarded all that. He had already made his decision. This buck had to be faced. Hopefully, that confrontation would occur soon, but no matter how long it took to locate him, the appointment had to be kept. This buck was a part of the puzzle which had to be solved.

So, he ate. He hadn't eaten adequately in quite some time, but he carefully followed an inner monitor which indicated the amount of acorns that he should eat. He had decided to spend the night resting relatively near the cedar rub. After all, maybe the offending buck would end up coming to him during the darkness to check up on things. If that was the case, then Nethanel would stand to benefit from an element of surprise. But it would also mean an immediate battle, and if he consumed too many acorns now, it could have a detrimental effect on his ability to destroy his opponent. So, he carefully ate just enough to restore his energy reserves to a safe level, and no more. Once he had done that, he then moved back into the softwood patch to a position where he could, from time to time, keep an eye on the rubbed cedar and its immediate surroundings.

Nethanel didn't sleep very well that evening but he was able to curl around some flitting dreams after a fashion. When the quiet reminder of a nervous thrush gently separated him from his dreaming world at first light the next morning, he realized immediately that he had done the right thing. An amazingly fit animal anyway, the night's rest had, in a most spectacular way, restored Nethanel to a state of good confidence, which he hadn't even realized that he had almost lost. He had become so absorbed with making his march to the north that he had failed to recognize how close he was to losing the physical ability to make that march and still have the wherewithal to take care of business once that march had ended.

So, unwittingly, the rival buck up above him had given Nethanel a great gift. The rest had been much needed. Once he was fully awake and totally focused on the immediate task at hand, Nethanel then arose from his bed to repay his new friend for the kindness which had so unintentionally been provided. By way of stretching, Nethanel mutilated a few more sizeable trees around his bedroom. Then he began the process of casting about to locate the buck responsible for bringing on this unseemly, though beneficial, delay.

Of course, Nethanel had a general idea where he needed to head, but the area in question was substantial to say the least. At this junction between the coastal plain and the mountains of western Maine, large foothills rose up from the plain. Interspersed between these foothills was a liberal amount of swampland which tended to make short distances long ones, even for white-tail deer used to such obstacles. Nethanel guessed that his rival spent most of his time at the top of one of these hills scattered around him. He based this assumption solely on the girth of the cedar rub that he was now rapidly leaving behind him. It took a wide rack to make such a rub, the wide rack of an open woods buck. To Nethanel, it seemed reasonable to believe that his rival would make his master bedroom at the top of one of these small mountains piercing the sky around him.

However, the prospect of having to search even a few of these good-sized hills was beginning to affect Nethanel's sunny disposition. Then he noticed something. Off to his right, heading in the opposite direction that he was now going, he caught the cautious glimmer of movement that he long ago learned to recognize. It was a doe. She was moving in that telltale fashion which spoke eloquently of purpose, of unwavering determination.

As luck, or fate, would have it, this was the undisputed matriarch of this region, and she was just starting to heed the bubbling of her annual heat. Though yet a few days off, the imminent arrival of her passionate crisis was utterly directing her steps when the appearance of Nethanel caused her to alter her gait. She made moves to avoid getting any closer to this formidable, strange new buck.

Nethanel did not press the issue. Even if he had detected an actual condition of white-hot heat, he would not have pressed the issue, at least not too much at any rate. But he could tell that such was not the case. He could tell that she was a matriarch, and that her time of heat was near, but that it was not there yet. So, painful as it was, he had to be patient. She was going to a place that mattered, a place where she and Sertorius had successfully, and safely, mated before. No other buck could have her. Of that Nethanel was absolutely certain.

So Nethanel hung way back, making sure he didn't alarm her or otherwise cause her to alter her destination. After a while she would care less about what was going on behind her. The big deer shadowing her was maintaining a very respectful distance, and he showed no signs of belligerence whatsoever. In fact, once in a while, as she calmly meandered along, once in a while, from behind heavy cover she would even glance back to see if Nethanel was nervous about anything.

Nethanel had played his cards just right. When the doe's forward progress began to peter out, he let her be. Obviously, she was not in heat, according to her body language. She had taken him as far as she was going to. However, because he had not forced her, she had inadvertently narrowed the cone of exploration that he would have to investigate in his search for the whereabouts of Sertorius. All he had to do now was place a bet. He could afford to gamble some time away, because he had secured himself an ace in the hole: a highly desirable matriarch ready to come into heat any day now.

Directly above him and slightly to his left, there were two mountains in evidence. He would now explore the one which seemed the most promising. Nethanel could cover hills of this size quite quickly. If he didn't come across the buck in a relatively short period of time, then he would simply return to the doe. He simply couldn't afford to obsess for very long on the whereabouts of Sertorius. After all, for all he knew Sertorius could have fallen to the shin-fa or the coydogs. Anyway, if Sertorius was gone, then the doe would be his by default.

Doubting this to be the case, Nethanel headed out for the nearest mountain in front of him. He was about a third of the way up its height when a prevailing northwest breeze occasionally carried a sound to him. Below him and off to his right was a lesser hill then the one he was on. It was sort of an offshoot of the mountain he was currently standing on, but it was a diminutive mountain in its own right. He could almost see the entire summit which consisted of ledge covered with low hemlock, scrubby pine and oak. Behind that summit there was a sizable gap or gully which was funneling a big brook down from a highland plateau to the flatlands to the south. That was the sound he was hearing from time to time when the wind shifted just right. It was a waterfall.

The waterfall had gotten his attention, but it was the large scrubby oak perched on those warm, sunny ledges which turned him around. Those comfortable, cozy ledges were just the right, discreet distance for a big buck to stroll from when a lady's need made itself evident. The more Nethanel stared at it, the more he became convinced that he was on to something. Those cozy granite outcrops, surrounded by good cover, with adequate food and water nearby, could only spell one thing: bedroom. Nethanel headed back downhill.

Though vaguely connected, it was still very rough country between the two foothills. To get from point "A" to point "B" he had to pass through a jagged gorge which made him turn out from time to time. Still, within half an hour Nethanel had emerged from the roughest places and was looking for the easiest way to get up the bedroom hill. While doing this he was careful not to expose himself to open areas where a stray shin-fa might be lurking. The open ledges above had been caused by the action of the glaciers scraping off the top of the hill and leaving a substantial boulder field down below. Though not entirely open, there was nevertheless a good deal of visibility here between the small trees and bushes. However, though the terrain called out for caution, once he got to the actual base of the lower hill, Nethanel became more convinced than ever that he had made the correct decision. He picked up his speed. The sound of the waterfall beyond the shallow mountain came to him more frequently and with a greater intensity as he went along.

A big buck, as much as possible, liked to have his back protected when he was resting and possibly even sleeping. The faint yet persistent sound of the waterfall told Nethanel that the ground just beyond the mountain was very rugged. Any danger emerging from that direction would come only rarely and would be easily detected by even a drowsy deer. Nethanel liked his chances and was soon rewarded by a welcome sight as he entered a dense fir thicket. He thought that he had glimpsed a fresh deer trail there, and he was at once heartened and yet instilled with an uneasy soberness by what he found at the beginning of the trail. It was what he wanted to find, and yet, now that he found it, his sense of discovery was tinged with as much fear as it was with joy. For there, nestled amongst the leaves of a nearby mammoth oak tree, there carelessly and casually spread out about the ground were the huge droppings of a truly dominant buck.

All was calm with the world of Sertorius. As the area doe came into heat one by one in an orderly fashion, no serious challenge had emerged from the local buck population. They had been well educated and knew their place in the pecking order. All knew that the important doe went to Sertorius.

The schedule was so firmly ingrained that even the matriarchs who were genetically inclined to breed late had taken to advancing their biological timetables. Why wait for something better to come along when an obvious king was firmly in place?

Sertorius was already acutely aware of a doe that mattered, just down off the mountain in her usual place. She was wise and would carefully wait until her heat was well established before she nestled up just a bit closer to where Sertorius was now resting. She was well satisfied with the progeny that Sertorius had visited upon her, and she saw no reason to alter a pattern of behavior which had worked so well in the past.

Sertorius was content with her judgement and waited for the breezes coming up the hill to announce to him that his little vacation was over. Thus, mollified and reduced to a state of near torpor by the warmth of the surrounding ledges, Sertorius was unprepared for the next turn of events. Basking in the mid-day sun, his drooping eyes were yanked open by a telltale sound followed almost immediately by an instantly recognizable scent. Far down the hill, right at the outer most limit of his vision, Sertorius caught a glimpse of movement. His vacation was over. He could tell that a deer was coming up the hill toward him and that it certainly wasn't the doe that he had been half dreaming about a few minutes earlier. His left ear promptly went to twitching and that twitching alerted Felix that something was amiss. The little fox then slipped off a discreet distance from where he had also been resting, to see what was coming up at them.

Sertorius did the same thing in his own way. Just down from the ledge where his bed was a narrow, level tract of soft, mossy soil lay in wait for Sertorius to use as an escape route if he felt there was a need to. Any buck of experience could see that this strip of mossy soil was the best way to travel along the face of this particular ledge.

Sertorius didn't tiptoe or sneak. Brazenly he leapt from his bed and sank his massive hooves into the soft soil right up to the dew claws, to depict a scene of panicked flight. However, once the mossy soil began to peter out when it merged with the surrounding ledge, Sertorius lifted his feet to a sneaking tread. When the soil finally gave out altogether and Sertorius was back on solid ledge, he didn't want any pieces of the soft dirt scattered about to indicate which direction he had gone in. Once safely, and cleanly, back on ledge once more, Sertorius got behind the cover of some young pine and then proceeded to double back to a grove of dense, low limbed hemlock which grew just above the spot where he had just been resting a few minutes before. Surprise didn't have to be total, it just had to be strategically placed. The trap was set with Sertorius holding the usual high ground.

Nethanel had seen something. There had been no noise, but he had definitely seen something. In theory it could have been anything—a squirrel, a turkey or a fox—but his adrenal gland was already kicking in. He knew.

The doe down below had already got the gears turning. Usually, close proximity to a doe in heat was the reason for average bucks to turn to combat. Though this particular doe wasn't technically in heat, she was close enough. These were not average bucks, and they needed scant reason to get down to business. The mere suggestion of sharing something as important as that doe was completely out of the question. And there was a lot more at stake than just her. Nethanel pinpointed where he had thought he had seen the movement, and then he unapologetically stomped up the hill toward that spot. Once he got up there, he realized that he was at or near the top of the mountain, because when he stopped stomping, the sound of the nearby waterfall came up to him with clear, unsullied sounds. With this sound coming up around him, he realized that he would not hear a distant deer running or slinking away, which, to him, seemed to be the case here as far as he could tell.

This bewildered and unsettled Nethanel momentarily. Then, however, just up ahead of him, he did in fact see the unmistakable evidence of a big buck running away. The mossy soil along the face of the ledge had given way during what was obviously a panicked departure. Though not entirely believing this convenient evidence, Nethanel nevertheless went over to cautiously examine the tracks to determine the speed and the direction that his rival had taken. With his head down and his line of sight following the path of Sertorius' apparent flight, Nethanel was startled when, down the hill and to his left, a young fox popped into view and emitted a sharp bark.

Absorbed though he was with this peculiar sight, Nethanel nevertheless had the presence of mind to react instantly to a soundless rush coming from the ledge up behind him. There, standing above him and wearing an expression which could only be described as a malignant leer, there was Sertorius. In an instant the leer took on a fixed, somewhat confused quality when Sertorius realized that his surprise appearance had no effect on Nethanel whatsoever. Occasionally, these theatrics yielded spectacular results in the form of foes being so unnerved that they would flee the scene forthwith, but not today. Sertorius knew he had to act immediately to salvage what he could of the element of surprise, coupled with the advantage of holding the higher ground.

Though Sertorius seemed to tower above him like a candlestick pine, Nethanel nevertheless lowered his massive antlers and prepared to climb up the ledge to cut his opponent down to size. Sertorius instantly advanced to prevent Nethanel from gaining any equal footing.

At the first twisting clash of the antlers, Sertorius realized that he had slightly underestimated the size of his foe. The length of Nethanel's body had successfully concealed his crouching height and weight, but Sertorius was not dismayed in the least. Though a massive beast himself, Sertorius had met, and defeated, several other bucks who had believed themselves to be nothing but untouchable. He had let his obvious smaller size work to his advantage. Not comprehending his stringy, ridge-runner physique, these larger animals had unwisely pressed what they thought was an overwhelming weight advantage. Once they fully committed themselves one way or another, it usually didn't take that long for Sertorius to drive them off balance. After that, the only question really left was whether or not their rear ends could stay away from the business ends of Sertorius' antlers as they escorted the defeated pretenders from the immediate, or not so immediate, territory (depending on how irate Sertorius happened to be at the given moment of retreat).

Nethanel made no such mistake. In fact, he was rather content with his position beneath the probing Sertorius. He kept threatening to let Sertorius surge past him, as the smaller buck twisted and jabbed with his rude rack. Nethanel could feel all too well his adversary's attempt move him toward a weak or unbalanced position.

Because of the reluctance of both parties to engage in an all-out effort, the fight proceeded to move laterally back and forth in an uneven, jerky manner along the face of the ledge. But that sort of stalemated, half-hearted jousting was destined to be of a very short duration. It simply didn't appeal to the better tastes of these courageous individuals; it simply wouldn't do at all. So, it really wasn't but a few minutes before the casual jousting suddenly gave way to some serious efforts at eye gouging and neck breaking. Every tine of both racks was fully squeezed and tested as the grinding heat of the battle began to lose all reason as the worlds of both bucks became engorged with a red rage that they could both literally smell and taste. Whoever lost this fight had better be prepared to run long and hard. Hard feelings were being permanently created. The need and desire to utterly destroy the opponent had taken root, as the moss on that ledge was violently torn asunder. Only death would satisfy now.

This was a lot to take in at once, but Sertorius was not dismayed. He saw his path to victory, and he had only to trick Nethanel into voluntarily striking down that road. As his breath hissed and blew above the harsh clacking of his massive antlers, Sertorius would occasionally take in the soft, leaf strewn softness of the ground behind Nethanel, just below the mossy ledge that they were now struggling on. If he could get his opponent down there and cause Nethanel to slip . . . well now, all kinds of good things could happen. These happy thoughts quickly merged into a coalescent plan which opened up to him almost as soon as he conceived it.

He had been shoving down on Nethanel since the fight had begun. Lately, he had begun to feel Nethanel attempting to time his shoves with a greater accuracy. It was obvious to Sertorius that Nethanel was waiting for that perfect shove which would allow him to quickly back off and let Sertorius more or less fall off the ledge in a clumsy manner. Sertorius could see that he wasn't going to push Nethanel from his current position. Down there, on the leafy, level ground, he would be in as much danger of losing his footing as Nethanel was. But he had faith in his agility, and, more importantly, Sertorius believed he could keep his ulterior motives completely to himself until the proper opportunity revealed itself. Without hesitation, he surged forward in an apparently desperate effort to force the issue.

When Nethanel felt the full force of the charge, he briefly met it, before giving way as a wrestler does when trying to draw an opponent off balance. He half suspected that something was up when Sertorius, perhaps a bit too easily, broke contact with his antlers and slid by Nethanel like a great brown snake heading for its den. Nethanel, guarding his flank from any passing blow as Sertorius headed down to the leafy flat, Nethanel was content to end the stalemate on the ledge.

Sertorius got to the level ground and whirled to prevent his own flank from being gored by the swiftly approaching antlers of his opponent. He had succeeded in assuming a good defensive posture. He would soon see if Nethanel had anything to offer in the way of equal opportunity fighting. Behind him, not that far away, was a precipitous drop off which fell some thirty-five feet down to the dark water of the pool beneath the waterfall that Nethanel had been hearing all that morning. It was loud enough now, with its nearness, that it effectively drowned out most of the sounds which were erupting from the clashing antlers of Sertorius and Nethanel.

The shallow, slippery soil on which they fought was being quickly torn to shreds. It had been raining heavily in recent weeks. That's why the waterfall behind them was so loud. The soil they were fighting on drained quickly and well, but there was still enough moisture in it to make footing treacherous once it was broken up. Any advantage Sertorius had been counting on was not materializing. Still, he was not dismayed.

The fight had been going on for some time now, so Sertorius decided that he could successfully feign fatigue. Craftily, he allowed Nethanel to back him off the battered soil of the leafy flat and up toward the edge of the precipice overlooking the waterfall. Nethanel didn't exactly know what was up there, but he could tell that there was a cliff of some sort just ahead. The prospect of shoving Sertorius off that cliff suddenly cheered him up quite a bit. It fired him right up, actually. He was the one who seemed to be leering now. The fact that Sertorius wasn't making a break for it and was instead apparently willing to be forced off a thirty-plus foot cliff didn't impress itself on Nethanel in the least. He didn't care how Sertorius was gone as long as Sertorius was disappeared. This certainty of victory made for a momentary letdown in Nethanel's intensity level, just as Sertorius seemed about to plummet down the precipice.

Suddenly, however, Sertorius caught hold of the right antler of Nethanel with the left side of his rack, and, with an act of sheer power that he had been saving for this crucial moment, managed to get Nethanel momentarily light on his feet as he attempted to shift positions against Sertorius. Feeling his advantage Sertorius gave a mighty twist of his neck and, as far as he could tell, succeeded in flipping Nethanel down toward the outermost lip of the cliff. Instantly, once Nethanel's body had gone past him, instantly Sertorius proceeded to whirl around to assist Nethanel in falling down over that cliff.

But the outer lip of the cliff was not a clear lip. Just below it were the remnants of ledge. On two such remnants, Nethanel stood crouched and coiled, waiting for Sertorius to come forward to push him off. Sertorius realized just in time that he had come forward too far too fast in his rash desire to destroy Nethanel. Nethanel, besides being a bit bigger than Sertorius, was also his equal in agility. When he had slid down the beginning of the face of the cliff, he was not dismayed. Nethanel was properly anchored when Sertorius surged toward him. He simply dipped down and prepared to skewer the exposed neck of Sertorius before flipping his opponent down off the cliff.

Sertorius wasn't prepared to see Nethanel in such a perfect defensive position. He had misread the lay of the land and had underestimated his opponent's athletic capacity. But he still had the presence of mind to realize what awaited him if he delayed in the least. Instantly, the fight had turned to flight, literally. When Nethanel erupted upwards with unexpected power to destroy whatever his antlers came in contact with, Sertorius reacted with a superb display of athleticism of his own. From a standing start, he floated upwards in a graceful arc as Nethanel's antlers soared skyward also. The neck and chest of Sertorius were never touched, though one of Nethanel's G-2 tines did roughly brush up against the region of his manhood as he passed over.

Without missing a beat, Sertorius managed to get his right rear hoof onto the last remaining outcrop of ledge and loft himself clear of the small trees growing from the cliff on his way down toward the pool below. As he fell, Sertorius noticed the whiteness of the shallower rocks and consequently did what he could to twist himself in a way which might allow himself to land into the darker, hopefully deeper, region of the pool. He had never done such a thing before, but when he entered the water, he instinctively pulled up to prevent himself from going too deep. It was a well-executed dive. Because of his defensive reaction, Sertorius only slightly grazed the slimy surface of a large, black rock on his way down into the deeper water. When he resurfaced and headed for the opposite shore, he was none the worse for wear.

Up above, Nethanel had mixed feelings when he saw Sertorius emerge from the pool unscathed. The thought crossed his mind, but in the end, Nethanel stayed where he was. He had no desire to duplicate his obviously defeated foe's feat. He understood that in all probability, Sertorius would remain on that side of the brook, permanently. He let the fire of his recent rage dissipate rapidly to prevent himself from rashly plunging after Sertorius.

While thus cooling down on the lip of that cliff, he was suddenly startled by the anxious whimper of a young fox not forty feet from him who had apparently been watching the whole proceedings. When Sertorius eventually emerged from the opposite side of the pool and prepared to wander away in defeat, the little fox promptly took off like a shot. In a few minutes, Nethanel saw him scurry across the top of the waterfalls and, soon thereafter, join up with Sertorius as the big buck left his home territory. With the waterfall serving as a visible and audible boundary line, Sertorius would never come back to that region of the forest again. What progeny he left behind, however, would be free to come and go and add greatly to the white-tail race.

–CHAPTER 11–
Merodach

All around him, inside and out, above and below, all around him the world swirled. Agitated, anxious, he pushed on, seeking he knew not what. The intensity of his despair was shocking in its newness. He had never experienced the world like this. He felt like he was being choked with an untethered, unbridled callousness which showed no sign of easing whatsoever.

The unrelenting agony of his condition had prodded him onward in aimless circles all morning as he sought some sort of relief from the bottomless emotions which now possessed him. Rail was beginning to lose hope as he meandered in bewilderment toward the nearby river bottom.

He had hoped that his search for the mushrooms, the physical exertion of it, would somehow lead him to a more peaceful, recognizable place. A blackness was drawing down all around him when he reached the bank of the river. The sun was sifting through the bright foliage of the trees that bent over the shallow water. They twisted in quiet circles as a light breeze followed the clear water downstream. Below the billowing shadows of the swirling leaves, the rocks beneath the water, both light and dark, revealed themselves in an oblique and obscure way as the trees shifted above them. *Maybe just like the face of the Almighty,* thought Rail, knowing that he had gone far enough down this path.

It wasn't much, but, just like the medieval folks with their imperfect mirrors in front of a skull, just like those people out of the shadows of history, Rail now at least had something he could take home with him to reflect upon and to remember.

When the matriarch of that region saw Nethanel returning from his fight on the mountain, she immediately went into heat. Traveling in small, ritualistic circles, she led the new boss buck on a token chase, just to be sure that he was truly fit to be her mate. She sensed that he was in a great hurry, but she had enough self-esteem to put on a fairly convincing display of coquettishness. Besides, she had to make sure that her biological chemistry was in fact dialed in to the proper level. An impatient shake of Nethanel's massive antlers convinced her that her level of receptiveness was as close to being perfect as it was ever going to be.

Nethanel knew that she was an important piece of the puzzle which had now seized control of his life. But as he rested the next day, he also sensed that if he lingered too long by her side that his entire life's mission could be in jeopardy. Usually after a buck mated with an important doe, he liked to sort of hang around to discourage lesser bucks from trying to dislodge his progeny through rough treatment of the doe in question. However, in this case, Nethanel didn't have the luxury of leisure.

As he looked off toward the higher mountains to the north, he realized that, as far as this particular doe was concerned, he would simply have to trust in her discretion and good judgement. The doe sensed that Nethanel was the top of the line, the very best that she could ever hope for. She would go into hiding and force the lingering effects of her estrus to subside as rapidly as possible. She could tell that the big buck by her side had pressing business elsewhere and that there was no need to hold him back. Their mating would be successful. Perhaps during the following years, if he survived, perhaps then their encounters would be less stressful and of a more leisurely nature. But for now, well, what do you expect of a buck anyways?

The restlessness of Merodach had dislodged most of his admirable qualities. This was difficult to do because Merodach had few, if any, admirable qualities. Undisputed ruler of a considerable portion of the northwestern badlands which lay just above the fertile agricultural regions of central Maine, Merodach had been blessed with a positive genetic outcome, at least as far as size was concerned. But he was also one of those rare individuals who combined the genetics of plenty with the genetics of want.

The central part of the state still held a certain amount of farmland, which guaranteed enough food to produce big deer on a consistent basis. Most deer were very reluctant to stray far from this proverbial horn of plenty, but nevertheless every once in a while, this big old icy wheel of perpetual contentment would peel off a splinter of itself toward the path of least resistance. In most cases this path would usually lead to the north.

In the south, the various activities of humanity had created a world of myriad edges where food and safety for deer could readily be found. The result of all this was that there were lots of deer and, generally speaking, large numbers of deer meant smaller deer. With that many deer around, there was not much need for the big deer of central Maine to go down there. Their size fit better with the vacuum which occasionally presented itself in the big woods that lay just to the east and north of the western Maine mountains. If a deer possessed a certain disposition, then that was a direction that they could consider.

The deep snow of the north woods made big size a necessity. There weren't very many deer there, comparatively speaking, but the ones that did thrive there had to be long legged and big. They also had to have an attitude, an edginess. They had to travel long distances to find food and mates. And when those attributes were located, they had to be defended vigorously. The bucks, therefore, were a bit more aggressive then was considered normal for the white-tail tribe in general.

The breeding of Merodach had accentuated this edginess to an extraordinary degree. Coming from an elderly, abnormally intelligent monster of a doe from the northern edge of the central region, Merodach had inherited all of her size and more. She had always been a spotty breeder, having produced only a handful of fawns in her lifetime. The Victorians would have said that she suffered from a delicate disposition. The farmers of early New England would have considered her "owlish." They both would have been right, but there was more to it than an emotional imbalance. There was a significant biological condition at work within her, also.

It is rare, but occasionally during hunting season a doe is harvested with a pair of horns adorning her noggin. Merodach's mother didn't have any horns on her head, but she did in fact have about as much testosterone coursing through her blood as she did estrogen. Merodach inherited more of the male side of her bearing then he did her female tendencies. This, along with what he got from his father, helped to make him an extremely belligerent individual.

His father, on the other hand, following his own version of white-tail madness, had swung low out of the deep north woods for one year and one year only. Whether he had intended this to be a one-year sojourn is hard to say, because the following winter, exhausted from his long trek, he had failed to survive a crusty snow coupled with an attack by the local coydog pack. Like his mother, the father of Merodach had not produced many offspring. Also, in a similar fashion, like his mother, the father of Merodach had blood which was too strong. He was a macho man's man. Most would describe him as vile, not virile, and violence seemed to be a necessity for him. This, along with what he got from his mother, made Merodach what some would consider an evil individual. As one of his last acts then, the father of Merodach delivered the bad seed which was his final son.

But it takes more than bad seed to create a malignant harvest. His mother, perhaps prompted by a genetic signal provided by Merodach's father, left her comfortable home in the south to teach Merodach that his destiny lay in the barren landscape to the north. That she was able to accomplish this task, even though she was a stranger to that region, was attribute to her intelligence and to her size. She did not back down from any matriarch that they came across. A big part of Merodach's nasty personality was created as he watched his mother cuff about the rightful owners of long held territories. This was not the norm, and Merodach enjoyed every minute of it. She definitely had a part in creating the bully that was to become Merodach.

It is said by some that in nature the uncommon extremes are always playing against each other to produce a common good, which, more often than not, usually expresses itself in the form of mediocrity. If one characteristic is emphasized too much by an individual or that individual's family, then chances are that that individual or that individual's family is apt to be a failure in the long run. But the extremes must always be tested, and Merodach personified a very dark extreme which is seldom seen, but is needed, nevertheless. When the rut was upon him, he had the size and the disposition to test the place of maniacal tendencies within the white-tail tribe.

In the gloom of the deep ravine he came. The swirling leaves gathered in portentous circles which succeeded in holding their secrets for the time being. Merodach had divined something in their scratchy whispering and had waited none too patiently for their thrashing to subside before advancing further. Once the whirlwind had sufficiently died down, he then picked his way through the blow downs and boulders before climbing up a steep knoll which guarded the ravine's upper entrance. Once there, Merodach had a clear view of the mountains to the west.

It had been three days since he had eavesdropped on the careless crows. Hidden in the scrubby hemlock of his favorite lair, Merodach had kept his eyes closed while his open ears absorbed the most interesting tidbits of the crows' gossip. Initially tangled in a mishmash of jealous raving, Merodach was able to overcome the difficult cadence of the crows' vocal code, just in time to decipher an event of grave importance. Filtering, weighing and adjusting the cracking rubric, which normally guarded the key to understanding their vocalizations, Merodach faked sleeping while listening with great interest.

Apparently, their ancient rivals, the ravens, had scored a great coup in the form of a feast which had lasted for days. Pushing aside the shrill clack of the agitated crows' description of the gory, gluttony of the hated ravens, Merodach was able to finally paint an accurate picture of an event which could mean a lot to him if he could figure out the appropriate response to that distant event.

He, his father, and an untold number of

his direct ancestors, had set in motion a cycle of apparent success. Circling, icy, sacrificing diversity with a distinct, dangerously inflexible agrarian certainty, Merodach, perhaps with the help of his father's maddened ghost, saw with startling clarity the futility of his current genetic situation. Helpless in this current stagnant certainty, Merodach and his progeny were destined to forever remain in that icy circle, until a change would either break them free or bind them forever to the frozen mass. Now came the crows with a tantalizing message. Perhaps a bit too abruptly, Merodach opened an eye and the terrified crows flew away, shrieking.

The great wheel of the white-tail world was in motion. An important gear in the nearby mountains had shifted and had left a vacuum there, for the time being. Sejanus, the long-time ruler of that region, had been eaten by the ravens. His power had been passed on, and now another buck had to answer the call to scale the peak of engagement which would lead to them meshing with the mystery which moved all things.

Merodach had never been interested in that place before. He had glanced at it occasionally, but a river nearby had been big enough to quell any rising curiosity that he might have entertained regarding that territory. Suddenly, however, the gossip of the crows caused that river to look like a brook. Any light arising in that region now needed to be filtered through Merodach's darkening presence. And it had to be filtered quickly. Another deer was heading toward that void. The crows had told him this, too.

It wasn't want which had driven her here, but plenty. And, more to the point, the complete absence of any of her kind which had magnified and exaggerated that plenty. She felt the young growing within her and she wondered, *Would the males come?*

When the young were born the following spring, would their thin cries reach back to attract the attention of those brave enough, strong enough, and intelligent enough to recognize the gleaming gears of opportunity? She had gambled that even if the males didn't actually descend on this area right away to claim it as their territory, that they would nevertheless still filter in close enough to make her gamble a success.

There was no reason for her not to succeed other than the dangers of isolation. Here, she was the lone star in the firmament. No nearby constellations of ancient family ties whirled to support and encourage her. Once there had been, but no more. Hunted to near extinction by the jealous and fearful shin-fa, her kind had fallen inward and away from their old places for many generations.

But there was plenty now. Plenty of game to hunt where the abandoned farms lay shadowed once again by the forest in the highlands. Shin-fa still moved around these places, but they didn't stay long. They had cut down most of the old trees, and the fresh, new, tender trees sprang back thicker than ever. And, as always, with these young trees came the deer. First to browse on those tender shoots and then when the surviving shoots grew into mature trees, then to gorge themselves on the mast crops which occurred from time to time. The coydogs also prospered here, taking their share of the deer, but plenty begot plenty, and, good year or bad, the deer numbers grew.

The shin-fa had forgotten her kind; but she, being one of the first and therefore one of the most important, she did not forget the shin-fa. Traveling at night she found the most remote remaining corridors of wilderness. Staying to them, picking her spots and taking as little chance as she could, she crossed tar roads only when absolutely necessary. Eventually she made her way, first to the dirt roads, and then finally to the highest hills which held only vague traces of long-ago abandoned logging trails.

Once there, she rested and then took the time to fully explore the avenues which would connect her to the steep, craggy regions which had no trails or roads whatsoever. She found the springs, the caves, and the most ancient deer trails which had been established shortly after the end of the last ice age. In a world of apparent nothing, she had found a safe haven right at the doorstep of unbelievable plenty. *But would the males follow?*

Nethanel thought he knew exactly where he had to go. Ahead of him lay a contorted mass of jumbled mountains and demi-mountains. Towering here, sloping there, the whole region looked like something that had been torn open by a monstrous dung fork and turned over unceremoniously. But Nethanel felt he knew where he had to go. In the way of his kind, his mother had given him a lot of the information he needed right at birth. But that was an incomplete perfection at best. Actually, getting to the designated place would be entirely up to him.

The closer he got to his destination, however, the more he came to realize that he was expending a considerable amount of energy resisting the danger of being too hasty. The effort required to practicing patience at this juncture was beginning to wear on him almost as much as fighting rival bucks did. Still, though the time of leisure was well past, Nethanel understood that now, more than ever, he had to be careful.

With Sertorius effectively set to one side, Nethanel no longer felt the need to worry about other bucks, even if they were animals of considerable merit. To speed things up he carefully took the time to skirt the areas of what would obviously be contested by cantankerous locals. They would have to be dealt with later.

Nethanel was no longer a line buck in the traditional sense. He had absolutely no intention of returning to the region from whence he had come. A prize was up ahead and from her would sprout the foundation of all his remaining efforts in life. If successful, she would provide the first stitch in a new, important piece of a fabric which had been evolving for over three and a half million years. Like a geode loaded with precious gemstones, Eloua had been hidden away until such a time that the wheels of millenniums would gently turn their lights to reveal the true nature of her worth. She was the tip of a gear which had arisen from the dark vaults of time.

Eloua was the last fawn of the mighty Sejanus. Her mother's grandmother had, in fact, been part of a line which was directly responsible for producing the worthy Sertorius. Eloua was a large, unusually beautiful doe who was lucky to be alive at all. Her mother, old and desperate, had sought out Sejanus in his remote domain. The great buck was about to meet an untimely demise, but not before he managed to bestow his greatest gift to the white-tail world.

Coming from an older parent should have doomed Eloua to mediocrity, but such was the strength of the blood of Sejanus that she was, instead, set up for a mysterious greatness. It was perhaps because of the presence of her blood in Sertorius which had caused Nethanel to seek him out so earnestly. Like her father, Sejanus, Eloua had traveled a lot in her lifetime, but now that urge had abated. She sought out a calm, remote place and opened up all that was within her to announce to any who mattered that an avatar of undeniable consequence had arrived.

Through the mother, Nethanel had been given his path and also through the mother, through the womb, some of his choices had been pre-ordained. She had provided him with his ship, with the structure that had enabled him to pursue his murky quest, but nothing would be clear until he heard the siren call of Eloua. Once he found her then his real life could begin.

Merodach had no prime directive to guide him through an unfamiliar territory. Instead, he depended on a reliable inner wantonness to sift through various impulses which swept over him as he emerged from the cold river which had heretofore served as his territorial boundary. He knew that something was up and that was enough, for now.

The crows had given him the bit and now he seized that bit with a brute contempt as he headed into a place that he knew not. At first, even he was a little hesitant, but soon the black wind which blew the leaves was providing a kind of shining which all of his type were able to utilize in lighting a path which led to an even darker shining. Like a black hole, soon that shining acquired a magnetic pull which would not destroy those of Merodach's ilk but, would instead, provide them with solace and, eventually, a direction to follow.

Late that afternoon he saw the mountains which would provide the shadows that he would need to absorb in order to home in on his quest. That night he rested in quiet darkness and listened for the guttural sounds of the ravens whom he hoped would still be gloating from the feast that Sejanus had provided. None came, but as Merodach slept, a dream came to him and alerted him to the sinister tugging which had theretofore been responsible for directing his life force.

At the earliest breaking of dawn, he awoke refreshed. Though the previous night's dream had been fleeting and vague, he nevertheless felt prepared to receive the conclusive tokens that the day, he was absolutely sure, was about to deliver to him. The ravens apparently were a long way off and not inclined to divulge any further information to him that would help him in this strange land. Rested and unperturbed, however, Merodach allowed the malignant tugging that his dreams had set in motion to ease forward into the vast internal whirlwind which would first draw in, and then skillfully winnow out, all the pertinent information that the surrounding countryside provided. If the overt darkness of the selfish ravens wouldn't help him, then the muted disappointment of the forces of light would have to inadvertently be his guide. The faithful chickadees and the stalwart red squirrels, who had stood by Sejanus through thick and thin, still quietly honored his memory when the sunshine was bright against the cloistered hills of his home territory. But their subdued, careful devotions threatened to tear apart all the intricate contributions which Sejanus had so courageously bequeathed to the white-tail race.

Emerging from the moldering swamp, Merodach unleashed the poisonous tentacles of his inner whirlwind and promptly picked up on the lingering disappointments yet emanating from Sejanus' admirers still living in the surrounding hills. Merodach's inner compass vacillated, hesitated, and then, like a heavy weathervane being seized by a stout northeast wind, the piercing, sharp blade of the weathervane's arrowhead was brashly thrust toward the direction he would confidently tread that day. So convinced was Merodach of the information he received that he even took the time to seek out an eight-inch poplar tree which stood by itself just of the first slight rise coming up out of the swamp. Lowering his dark, massive, open woods rack, he ripped at the tree with undisguised glee and anticipation. When he came to the prize ahead, he would brook no interference from any of the lesser local bucks who might be entertaining false notions of greatness.

Occasionally the wind came right to hear a noise above the sound of the waterfall. Zadoc, being the oldest, was sent out by Athaliah to investigate the result of a fight between two massive bucks. Not wanting to interfere with a potential free feast, Zodac had stayed downwind and a respectful distance from the fracas going on in the woods above him. *Who could tell?* If everything went right, one of the deer could be savagely gored or otherwise rendered happily helpless. These things happened, and no self-respecting coydog could afford not to check out a potentially well-placed tragedy. No need to work any harder than you had to.

Hell, if things went really well, there would be no work whatsoever. All you'd have to do is give a few high-pitched barks, and the whole pack could just walk up to a deceased, warm white-tail behemoth, casually tear him to pieces, and then proceed to continuously chow down until everything—meat, bones and hide—was completely devoured at a very leisurely pace. In the end that was, after all, the name of the game:

getting the utmost amount of food with the least amount of energy.

When Zodac could finally clearly make out the unmistakable clicking of the bucks' antlers as they twisted and turned against each other, then he began to carefully work up the hill, until he achieved the best vantage point he could get. The young fir and hemlock made this difficult, but he didn't want to spook the fighting deer in any way. The longest fights sometimes yielded the best gored bucks. If they were left entirely to their own devices, there was always the hope that during the struggle their antlers might lock and thereby doom both the bucks to their deaths. As this usually happened only to big bucks, then the locked horn scenario could realistically yield a meal somewhere north of four hundred pounds. Needless to say, Zadoc couldn't wait to see how the fight ended, but he had to be patient and let nature take its course.

So, even when the clicking antlers grew steadily louder, indicating a very intense fight indeed, even then Zadoc stayed well-hidden and shifted around in the heavy brush to make sure that the deer didn't catch wind of him. It was a long fight, however, and finally the turning of the breezes forced him out along the edge of the river just above the waterfall. The flow of the air was more consistent there.

Suddenly he could actually see the combatants struggling in a very precarious manner on the edge of the cliff above the falls. Surely, it seemed to Zadoc, surely this had to end badly for somebody up there. Then, when Sertorius performed his top-notch dive down into the pool below the falls, then and only then, did Zadoc get up and slink out into the open to hopefully get a better view of the damage that surely had to befall the stricken Sertorius. But then a strange smell that stirred his ancestral ghosts momentarily immobilized him. Then, stricken with blinding fear, he bolted from that place to seek the safety of the pack, the safety of numbers.

If the natural world concerned itself with such things, then the running of Zadoc could have been seen as a signal that a fine tipping point was ushering in the very beginning of a new epoch for Nethanel and his kind. But no living thing overly concerns itself with such fine points when struggling to overcome the sound and fury involved with prolonging their existence.

Nethanel, for instance, was extremely

content to drift along, while Zadoc and his pack vacated this particular part of the forest for what ended up being a rather extended period of time. It was only much later, years later, that necessity forced them to take their chances and reluctantly attempt a reentry into this region. It was a numbers game as usual. When their numbers were low, they got out. When the numbers in the pack grew too high, then losses became acceptable.

But ignorance is bliss, and at this particular time, with the near emasculation of Sertorius so recently warming his rutting heart, at this particular time, Nethanel was as blissful as a buck in his position could possibly be. Whenever he came close to local bucks completely out of their minds with the passions of the season, Nethanel would blithely circumnavigate their areas of influence in an act of deferred gratification.

Later my friends, he chortled to himself, *Later I'll deal with you.*

Eloua was somewhere not all that far ahead, and Nethanel was in a deer's version of love. Short on romance perhaps, but a love nevertheless, bristling with an immensely unyielding purpose. Something beyond his normal, selfish, self-centered limitations was coalescing itself into a state of thralldom which actually excited him beyond anything that he had ever experienced before. Only an animal possessed of his courage and rank could endure this sensation without going mad and dying that way.

Nethanel channeled it all into a calm which allowed him to move with a lightness and freedom that he would never feel again. What would have destroyed others only promoted an orderly alignment of all his powers to blend in with all the positive charges, seen and unseen. The magnet pulling him was perfectly matched by the steel within him that had been placed there by his mother and all the wombs of the white-tail world, now and forever.

It didn't matter if his current direction wasn't perfect. Something, he knew, something would tweak and fine tune his path. Eloua would guide him, because she had been given the power to do so. He felt that any danger coming toward him now would only guarantee his ultimate success. Therefore, without further delay, Nethanel headed southeast.

Merodach, meanwhile, once he had penetrated as deeply into the first serious set of the western mountains as far as he felt necessary, swung to the south. All the information that he was receiving from all his old reliable sources indicated that he was on course. As this was his first endeavor at being a line buck, however, there was a certain hollowness in the pit of his stomach which took some time to master and overcome.

He had plenty of time to do so. The place he decided he needed to go to was well guarded by a serious series of deep, difficult, gouged-out ravines, which were periodically reinforced by the steep, shaggy shoulders of competing mountains, any one of which were ten times the height of the largest hill in his home territory.

Despite his best efforts, he soon found himself longing for the old ice circle which had kept him and his ancestors isolated and safe since the end of the last ice age. It, the ice circle, twirled like a dull saw blade in the darkest part of his jaded heart. Merodach knew that he was in great danger out here in this exposed environment, but his perverse pride strongly rebelled at notion of retreat. How could he humble himself now? To what would he return to and what grace could he lean on if he were to return in failure to the hollow home from which he had so recently and vaingloriously departed from? So, in the end, he hardened his heart and dug his way up, out of yet another endless cascade of crumbling, ancient blow downs and past the myriad boulders of all shapes and sizes which had fallen down the steep slopes of yet another nameless mountain.

Needless to say, progress was slow. If he had known the country through which he was passing, then his journey would have made a lot more sense than it was currently making. But the thin clouds which had been gathering overhead all morning had unmistakably hardened into a great grey sail which confidently seized hold of his sinews and lifted him triumphantly from summit to summit as the distance between him and his goal shortened, despite all the obstacles.

At last, he glimpsed the long shoulder of one of the otherwise ubiquitous mountains which had all been threatening to crowd him down the ravine of a waking nightmare. But this shoulder seemed as exposed, as vulnerable, and easily accessible as any naive young doe who had ever breathed the air of earth. Through the ever-darkening light of the now approaching autumn storm, the shoulder of this particular mountain, with its beech and oak stands gleaming as with oil, beckoned coyly to him even as he insulted its innocence with his brash and arrogant advance.

Garrius was the largest cock partridge in the immediate vicinity of Nethanel's latest travels. There were others of considerable size around the territory he had occupied, but he was the biggest, and he held the best spots. Holding the best spots by the best birds was the main reason that the partridge population was no longer bothered by any prospects of extinction.

And, by any reasonable measure, extinction could easily have been a concern for any species that did not possess the degree of adaptability that was held by the partridge. Every area was different, but in the land that Garrius lived, there had been three factors of high stress which had been successfully overcome by these resourceful birds.

First of all, came the loss of habitat. The winters in this part of Maine were more severe than down on the coastal plain, but there had been a lot of farming here which provided biological edges for partridge to survive in, especially around the fairly significant apple orchards. When the hard-scrabble farming of New England moved out to the smooth lands of the mid-west, the old pastureland in Maine eventually returned to the forest. These forests provided mast crops and other types of forage, but the flocks of partridge had to disperse more and take on a different nature in terms of size and intelligence.

It really wasn't so long after all that occurred that the coydogs came onto the scene. Partridge always did have plenty of critters preying on them. Domestic cats, bobcats, fox and various birds of prey all saw fit to chow down on the tasty ruffed grouse whenever the opportunity presented itself. The coydog took all that to a new level. First, the rabbits and then the partridge took the brunt of coydog hunting efficiency very hard at first. However, once the weak and the stupid were weeded out, both rabbit and partridge numbers recovered, though always to a lesser degree then what they had been.

On top of all this, the partridge had one more significant obstacle to overcome. Sometime after the arrival of the coydog, the turkey was introduced to the forests of Maine. Turkeys eat about anything: fruit, bugs, snakes, and the young of some species, like partridge. Again, the number of partridges declined until only the birds with the most admirable qualities were left. Basically speaking, partridge now had to be physically big and paranoid to an extraordinary degree.

Garrius had both these attributes to the highest level possible in his kind. Any buck worth his salt would learn to heed the thunder coming from the frightened wings of a bird like Garrius. His weight and unusual size made navigating in flight, through the thickets that he liked to hang out in, a difficult act that would only be taken, only if it were absolutely necessary. If Garrius sensed that there was any danger about, then he would tiptoe in his waddling way toward some sort of drop off or ridgeline with a ravine or hollow on the other side. That way once he was finished with his thunderous takeoff, he could then glide for a long time if he wanted to.

On this particular day, Garrius had been happily salvaging some beech nuts, when a feeling of trepidation came over him. He quietly got himself to the edge of a granite shelf where a large bunch of young beech gave him the confidence to wait out this feeling of unease. He didn't mind false alarms because, in his own way, he knew that in this remote territory a lot was riding on his staying alive.

Just below him a small brook ran noisily from a freshening rain the night before. Any sound coming toward him would be muffled. The morning sun, which only minutes ago had been sharp and bright, was suddenly overtaken by a thin screen of newly arriving storm clouds. In spite of that thin screen, just as he was contemplating a return to the beech nuts, a discernible, though unfamiliar, shadow fell over him. But then Garrius was jolted by a memory emerging from the vault of his ancestral past. Without further ado, he blasted from the cover of the young beeches and swiftly drifted down through the ravine below.

All that morning Nethanel had been feeling as though he, also, was being stalked. Before long he took to hiding in thick groups of young fir, watching for long periods of time the trail from whence he had just come. The less he saw, the more concerned he became, and, after a few efforts of detection in this manner, with the trees hiding everything but his eyes, Nethanel became distressed to a very high degree.

At first, he suspected a nefarious, malignant shin-fa of advanced age and experience of being the culprit responsible for bringing on this unease, this vast disquiet. But the silent hushes, oozing in an almost continuous, barely audible whimper from the forest, first only from the back, and then, as the morning crept on, then from the woodland all around him, the silent hushes began to take on an increasingly ominous portent. It was as though the world he was familiar with was shrinking back in horror and disbelief.

Finally, as he shifted round the protecting shoulder of a steep, dark mountain, finally came the smells. Nothing overtly obvious, for the route he was traveling was lacking in wind speed and direction, because of that hill which towered over him and effectively shut him in. Only the occasional rush of moisture from the slow, lethargic rise and fall of air going up and down the shadowy vastness of the mountain slope, now and then, provided the faint hint of a scent he strongly felt that he should know.

The smells that came to him evoked a whirlwind of ghosts and unpleasant sensations. He continued stopping and checking behind himself much more frequently then he normally did under those circumstances. Finally, when the sense of unease began to turn into a feeling of actual panic, finally he became convinced that he was making a serious mistake stopping so often.

He didn't exactly break into a run or anything like that, but Nethanel did force himself to glide steadily forward for much longer periods of time, before now and then halting to listen and smell.

Every time this precautionary activity revealed no tangible evidence of anything amiss, the tension of his inner anxiety was not relieved but only wound inexorably tighter. Still, with no solid proof to go on, Nethanel felt compelled to hold to the course that he was currently committed to, until something concrete convinced him to alter that course.

Garrius exploding from out of the young beech behind and above him was all the evidence Nethanel needed to radically alter his current demeanor. The big partridge had been quite a way in back of him, but Nethanel felt the panic emanating from the beating wings of the wily veteran. Clearly all was not well, and whatever had caused the old grouse to vamoose so suddenly and so unceremoniously from the immediate vicinity was reason enough for Nethanel to vamoose as well.

The bird was gliding rapidly at what he felt was a sufficient altitude, when he suddenly banked much harder to the right then he had wanted to. That was because, as he passed over Nethanel, the mighty buck unleashed one of his greatest leaps when he cleared a large rock, nearly impaling Garrius as he did so. Nethanel scaled the shaggy shoulder of the mountain, which had been hemming him in all morning, in just a few minutes, with the intention of putting as much real estate as he could between himself and that ravine. He had given up on the direction which he had been going. From now on he would go due east over the roughest terrain he could find.

Rail was reasonably content with the ground he had covered that day. He hunted by checking the land. There were certain places that during certain times during the deer season that he would plan his day around. His restless nature prevented him from sitting or standing for very long, so he still hunted, preferably alone. What some hunters would cover in a forenoon would require a full day for Rail to survey to his complete satisfaction.

Looking ahead as he snuck along, Rail would pick out a tree that he could lean against. The tree had to be smooth and offer a reasonable open view of the land ahead. Very seldom did he see a deer coming toward him, but once in a while by sneaking carefully in this manner, he could get close to a group of deer and jump them. He rarely shot at running deer, but if there was a deer with antlers among these scattering deer, then he knew what he would do. He would let them run away in an apparent easy escape. Then, after a few minutes, he would step to his left and pretend to follow them, making no efforts to conceal his movements. However, when he got behind some big boulders or heavy cover, he would carefully and quietly turn around and go back in the direction that he had just come from. Once he figured that he was out of their sight, then Rail would hustle (for him) far around to his right, in a large circle, until he was somewhere near where he had originally jumped the deer. Then he would, in fact, sit for sometimes two or three hours. It wasn't foolproof, but this hunting technique had worked for him in the past.

He hadn't jumped any deer with horns on this day, but he had nevertheless gone over the ground that he had intended to cover. Because of that he was reasonably satisfied with this day's hunt. Now it was time to head for home. His hair had grayed considerably in just a year's time. This didn't concern him in the least. He was content with the emotional level he had achieved for himself recently. He had addressed all the places he had wanted to survey that day, and he was still feeling at peace with himself as he approached the region, the space, that he had been in that black afternoon one year earlier. As a matter of fact, that small river which had so concerned him that day was not that far from where he was standing now. The sun was still high on the tops of the shorter trees, so there was no need to rush. He felt confident in going back down there again and getting out before darkness ruined the view.

Merodach was a divergent force of nature. Nothing was going to stop him. Neither bullet nor horn was going to deter him from following the direction which was now laid out before him. He was shielded by an invisibility that was granted to his kind to ensure the moving forward of exotic plans that he, himself, cared nothing about.

In the old dowel mills of that region, the shin-fa who worked there had tools which helped to keep them on their toes. Wielding these tools enabled them to subdue a place in the wild world in which they lived. Wide, dark brown and dangerous, the bolter saws' keen white teeth moved with an undeniable invisibility that gave no quarter. In a similar fashion, Merodach was the leading edge of an icy circle of the generations of deer who had created him. Absorbing its incessant, dark brown twirling, Merodach easily sliced the distance between himself and the soft slope of the luminous mountain where Eloua was hiding, according to his sources. She might not be biologically ready for his advances, but he would soon convince her to step up her timetable, or else.

Once he had gained a firm foothold on that languid slope, Merodach wasted no time in thrashing some otherwise stout poplar to announce his arrival. The light from the setting sun was directly hitting that part of the forest at that time. It slid off the dark beams of his antlers as he grimly made his way uphill, lending an ominous portent to his every step. Soon the outer members of Eloua's impressive entourage made themselves apparent, before they melted away to form the main body of a phalanx which Eloua had sent forth to somehow delay the inevitable arrival of Merodach.

But Merodach was in no mood to be delayed. One more time he rang the doorbell. Picking out a nine-inch pine tree, he took great pleasure in stripping off a patch of its soft, sticky bark. Gouging it a little for good measure, he then stood back momentarily to admire his handiwork. Then, with much violence, he pawed at the ground twice before heading up the hill.

After putting a rugged mountain between himself and what he felt was imminent danger, Nethanel then resumed his journey in an easterly direction. He soon found a large brook which, after passing the adjoining shoulders of two mountains, quickly transformed itself into a robust free stone river. Here it was flat enough to make for easier going although he was still somewhat disorientated by the panicky message of the terrified Garrius.

Eventually, Nethanel convinced himself to slow down to a more manageable, safer pace. He was traveling on a large highland plateau which was gently turning the river eastward. Though not at all sure where he should be heading, Nethanel was nevertheless calm as he picked his way along, confident that his inner steel would soon tip his internal compass toward the right direction.

Rail descended toward the river down an old tote road which had originally been bulldozed out of a steep hill on his right-hand side. When he initially headed down the "ramp road," as he called it, Rail had a largely unimpeded view of the flat below. The river was a hundred yards or so out to his left as he came down the hill, preoccupied somewhat, but still maintaining a good hunting posture as he descended. He was looking for the exact spot on the river's bank that had affected him so profoundly the year before. Again, where the ramp road entered onto the flat, the spot he was thinking of was upstream to his left. Afterwards, he realized that this was what had cost him in the end.

All the way down the ramp, he had had good visibility through the flat and even beyond, across the river. Now however, as the road ended and blended in with the flat, now there was an extended line of young hemlock of varying size which began to inhibit his visibility. Unconsciously, his good hunting posture began to suffer, as he sought to focus on the river beyond this hemlock. Rail hadn't seen anything for several days running, and he saw no particular reason to suspect that he would see anything now. It wasn't late but the quality of the light was strongly starting to turn the other way, from early afternoon to midafternoon. He still had a fair step to go before he could stretch out to the warmth and comfort of home and hearth. With the hemlock guarding his approach, he slid down the remaining distance of the ramp road to the beginning of the flat proper.

While he was doing that, he kept his eyes firmly focused, as best he could through the dense hemlock, toward the spot upstream which he intended to go to. It just so happened that while doing this, he noticed something. He halted his progress immediately and swore fervently under his breath. He didn't know what to do now. While looking upstream he had noticed a small movement on the other side of the river, up beyond where he had been looking. He knew instantly what it was, and he could only agonize, as he wondered whether or not the discovery had been mutual. The place where he was standing was unacceptable. He absolutely had to inch forward a few feet to get to a place where he could gaze through the hemlock screen in an effective manner.

Searching through the screen presently in front of him, Rail sought to determine whether he could safely move forward without giving himself away. At such moments, all a hunter can do is gamble. To stay where he was would be futile. He slid carefully forward to a place where he could at least have some sort of visibility. About that time a monstrous, grotesquely huge buck flipped into full view before sliding behind a narrow clump of three, ten-inch white maples. Beyond those maples were clear, obscenely unimpeded patches of open ground. Unconsciously, Rail had already raised his 308, and his heart was beating loudly as he waited for Nethanel to reappear. It took much longer than it should have before Rail realized that that buck was never going to come out on the other side of those slender maples.

Nethanel had seen the last movement behind the thick screen of hemlock. Rail had been careful, but just as he had stopped, Nethanel had made out the moment of Rail's left foot settling into place. It looked too dark for a squirrel, but Nethanel allowed for the remote possibility that the movement belonged to a bird. This cheerful thought crossed his mind, as he calculated the size of and distance to the clump of white maples that he was rapidly approaching.

He allowed the gait that he was traveling at to pick up imperceptibly. He had grave doubts about the squirrel or bird or whatever it was that he had seen across the way. He focused intensely on the clump of maples and willed himself to be behind them without appearing to panic. But he knew. He hadn't wanted to change direction, and he resented the intrusion, but he already knew.

Then, just before he dipped down into a shallow depression behind the maples, he caught the glimpse of another movement, which completely verified his paranoia.

Rail had been very careful to lift his gun up slowly. But through one small peephole in the hemlock canopy, Nethanel had nevertheless caught an unmistakable glimpse of the business end of a gun being raised. No mutant chickadee that black spot!

"Shin-fa!"

The full realization of his situation instantly flashed through Nethanel's mind. Without even remotely offering to hesitate, Nethanel got himself behind the clump of maples before turning sharply left and lowering his body as far as he could while still moving. Despite this awkward position, he began to move much more rapidly than he had before. As luck would have it, the shallow depression behind the maples turned into a short, narrow trough where eons of rainwater had exited from the depression. At the other end of this trough was a good-sized oak which lined up perfectly with the far left-hand side of the maple clump, at least from Rail's perspective.

Using this oak tree in conjunction with

the maple clump, Nethanel scooted around the bare, exposed end of a boulder-strewn knoll and, with a sudden burst of speed, soon found refuge behind a deceptively thin screen of young pine and beech. During this brief interval of two or three seconds, though he had been moving at top speed, he had not made one sound on the leaf-strewn surface. Once he got behind that screen of pine and beech, he immediately slowed to a crawl, though he never once stopped. This was a gamble. If there were other shin-fa with the one below, then they might get an effective look at him.

Nethanel's gamble paid off, however, and he was now headed due north. In front of him, about a mile and a half away, was the steeper side of a mountain shoulder which happened to line up with a rather long series of mountain valleys. Because of this lining up, this particular part of this particular mountain could be seen from many miles away. Nethanel was about to descend down a shallow ridge when something stopped him in his tracks. A faint knell of recognition awoke in him as he vaguely recalled standing on a similar ridge with his mother some seven years before. Suddenly, the shin-fa and the unease of the morning were forgotten. With a surge of inexplicable enthusiasm, he headed robustly toward the base of the mountain ahead.

Merodach had not been put off by the efforts of Eloua's attending does. What did they take him for, a rank amateur? Judging by their various reactions, it was all too apparent that the lady of the house was not ready to receive male visitors, especially rowdy ones.

Merodach was in no mood to be put off by such delicacies. It was clear to him that a bit of persuasion at the end of several of his well-placed tines was in order. Generally speaking, he had found that such behavior in the past had convinced a lot of hormones to be unceremoniously released by what had been supposedly reticent does.

With this in mind, he found a rather well-preserved logging road leading up the hill in the general direction that he intended to go. He then let his wagging well-worn tines be his guide from there out. With his nose a few inches from the ground, Merodach was accurately able to decipher Eloua's scent and the direction she was headed from among the myriad smells and paths which had been laid down by that matriarch's entourage. She was heading for the top of the hill.

After half an hour, the slope Merodach was climbing began to level off almost imperceptibly. The sun of the morning had given way to a shell-gray overcast which was deepening rapidly as a wet cold front approached from out the northwest. Despite the decreased light, the general visibility was actually better now without the glare of the sun bouncing off the white birch and beech trees which dominated this particular plateau. The plateau ran for a distance of about eighty yards, before it abruptly broke away from the gentle slope he had just come up from and then pitched sharply down the steep, southeastern side of the mountain. Just before he was fully upon the flatness of the last part of the plateau, a movement up to the right of Merodach got his undivided attention. Up beyond the flat, where the mountain jutted toward the summit, Eloua was busy making her escape from this aggressive newcomer. This caused a light line of blood red rage to creep into Merodach's vision as he witnessed this rather unapologetic rejection of his amorous overtures. Then, just as he was contemplating moving up after her, then came a movement off to his left.

Nethanel had also witnessed Eloua's attempt

to escape. He had been down out of sight on the steeper side of the hill just as he was approaching the beginning of the plateau where Merodach now stood. In her movements Nethanel recognized the presence of a distress which had not been brought on by his own approach. An adversary was clearly nearby, so he had hustled to get up to the flat ground and thereby achieve what he hoped would be equal footing for a change. He was relieved when he realized that he had accomplished this. If anything, he had the slightest advantage in elevation on this narrow platform, as he faced the massive buck now in front of him.

The look that passed between them was without rancor. Each of them recognized the immediate truth that total defeat and destruction was the only possible option here. There could be no passing off or sliding by, as the massive antlers weaved slowly back and forth on their way to each other. Positive and negative cannot exist in the same spot, and there would be no vacuum allowed at the point where these antlers would meet.

Unlike Crassus and Sertorius, who had relied on cleverness and guile to give them a crucial, slight advantage at the beginning of a potentially lethal confrontation, Merodach had always opted for the complete opposite effect when another big buck challenged his territorial imperative. Spreading his thick front legs far apart, Merodach slowly lowered his head to give Nethanel a prolonged look at a huge, bulging neck which was more than adequate to guide his gigantic rack toward every undesirable place imaginable. Though the base of this rack was quite dark, every one of its ten, gleaming points tended to have a distinctly hypnotic effect as they wended their way in Nethanel's direction. Nothing was hidden as Merodach confidently let his past history of total destruction build on an aura of violence and intimidation. Could this pretender not see that, in the end, he was completely overmatched and outdone?

Nethanel, on the other hand, had never postured nor put on airs. He was always very businesslike and somewhat analytical about his fighting. When it came to physical conflict, fear had never once entered into his thinking. If an adversary was in front of him, then the only thing left to do was to apply that which had been given to him by birth and fortune. The main thing given to him by these twin forces was the full weight of a somewhat benign hubris which was always guided by an inner, somber drumbeat very similar in substance to that which had been used to encourage the men manning the oars on Roman warships. This drumming, this beat within, kept his sense of *dignitas* in balance and always allowed his decisions, when it came to fighting, to be carried out with confidence and conviction. Nethanel heard this beating coming from within the inner sanctums of his fully opened heart as he stepped forward to accept the challenge of Merodach.

Instantly, things went badly for both of them. Their racks were both similar and dissimilar at almost exactly the wrong places. The mother of Nethanel had descended from a tribe which had originated in the Ohio valley area. Therefore, a part of Nethanel's rack wanted to be an open woods rack. However, his father, Essene, had been as deep a Maine swamp deer as had ever been created. And he had been a very dominant deer. Therefore, Nethanel's rack, despite some obvious signs of desiring to be an open woods rack, nevertheless swept in a magnificent clumsiness over the sides of his face in a good imitation of a swamp rack.

Merodach, on the other hand, coming from the central farmland of Maine, had a much more pronounced open woods rack. However, within that ancient ancestral region, liberally dispersed between the uncertain dry regions, were plenty of old fashioned, honest-to-goodness swamps which, like Nethanel, gave his rack a distinctive, though more attractive, bend over the top.

The trouble was these two racks didn't mesh very well, a fact that registered with both bucks almost immediately. Besides the obvious, awkward sensation of having a clumsy and dangerous dance partner, there was also an almost visceral revulsion with having to come to grips with the likelihood that a loss of eyesight or some other grisly injury could occur with such an asymmetrical union of antlers. So, while both bucks were more than willing and eager to get on with the task at hand, there nevertheless, was a rather extended period of feeling each other out to determine basically where there were tines to be avoided at all costs. This had to be done in a seamless, instantaneous manner by each respective combatant to avoid transmitting any vital information to the opponent. It simply wouldn't do to let the other guy know where one's weak spot might be. Any serious doubt expressed by either buck would be exploited to the maximum level by the foe in front.

As they were both veterans of many serious

fights, however, it wasn't long before the polite chit-chat came to an end. Without warning, both bucks simultaneously determined which directions and movements absolutely had to be guarded against while mounting a maximum attack themselves. The tinkling of reluctant tines instantly transformed itself into a sonorous, low sound of grinding beams which provided the bass notes for a deadly ballet.

Some intelligent, dominant bucks avoid unnecessary fighting as much as possible. That's partly because, once joined, there is no guarantee that massive antlers, forced together by the powerful thrusts and twists of their respective owners, each totally absorbed by a desire to vanquish their opponents, there is no guarantee that these antlers will not become permanently locked together. Once united in this fashion, there is no hope. Both bucks are doomed to die a terrible death.

The horns of Nethanel and Merodach did not mesh together cleanly. Nethanel was acutely aware that the narrow platform on which he and Merodach now skated upon was but a short distance from the steep, boulder-strewn slope that he had just struggled up through. He had to hold his position no matter what. So, grudgingly, he put up with the foul breath and rude thrusting of ill-placed tines which both seemed to be exploding from the powerful frame of Merodach.

Merodach, for his part, saw in the steep inhospitable slope behind Nethanel, the promise of a speedy cessation of hostilities if he could just figure out some way of forcing his opponent down into that happy abyss. Throwing caution to the wind, Merodach redoubled his twisting, grinding attack. He got nowhere, however, as Nethanel found good footing and lowered the neck of his opponent in the process. The massive antlers ground against each other and, for a few dangerous moments, proceeded to approach the locking point several times. A few thousandths of an inch either way would have spelt disaster for both of them. It was as if the horns were locking and unlocking almost at the same time. In a fraction of a second, one side would cement together just as some slight slipping on the other side of the rack would force a fortunate release.

One of Merodach's brow tines, which Nethanel had been finding most annoying and disturbingly close to his left eye, suddenly snapped off and lost a good inch of its length. There was no way that Merodach could put a positive spin on this development. At first, he had found Nethanel's obvious refusal to be intimidated an incredulous, almost absurdly foolhardy mistake that he intended to capitalize on in a businesslike, methodical manner. Let the fool stand there if he wished. This pretender would soon feel the painful humiliation of some well-placed tines in his rear end!

However, as the tortured minutes stretched forward into what seemed like hours, and the leaf-strewn ground around the narrow platform became increasingly chopped up and mutilated, however, it slowly began to dawn on Merodach that his well-placed confidence may have actually consisted of an ill-conceived arrogance. Being mistaken to this degree caused a deep rage to erupt within him, and so Merodach got low once again in an all-out attempt to throw Nethanel down the steep, wooded slope behind them.

Nethanel, because of the way his rack was built, had been fighting this battle "from above," as it were. Initially this position had been a cause for some considerable concern on his part. Though well dug in and able to hold his own, Nethanel nevertheless felt quite light on his feet and therefore somewhat vulnerable. However, when Merodach's brow tine snapped off, Nethanel could not help but feel that there had been a shift in the pulse of the conflict.

A sudden increase in the pressure on Nethanel's neck and hind feet, though it spoke of a panic and a justifiable fear which had evolved into a completely desperate effort to snatch victory from the mocking jaw of defeat and death, it, this pressure from Merodach, was now, in fact, threatening to successfully tear Nethanel's feet from the slender platform which had become the focus of his entire existence.

A low, dark rage swept over Nethanel's body as he grimly maintained this precarious perch. Though the day was not overly cold, vast streams of vapor escaped his nostrils as he shifted his antlers ever so slightly toward Merodach's broken tine in order that he might gaze down balefully into Merodach's maddened eye. Everything that Nethanel was became solidly concentrated into the bottom of his beating heart.

So complete was this concentration that finally, after some long minutes, finally, all Nethanel could hear was a subdued hissing sound. It brought back ancestral memories, memories of an ice sheet grinding ineffectually against the solid granite ledges by a long-lost ocean. In an effort to escape the vast, surrounding sheets of ice, many of his ancestors had grimly attempted to escape beyond the glacier by swimming along a string of coastal islands. In the end, most were not strong enough or brave enough to endure this trial. But some of them were. Some had measured up, had given everything and had survived to greet the next great wheel of evolution that was to shape their tribe. Nethanel had descended from this group.

Now, faced with the relentless pressure of Merodach's icy rage, now, as then, Nethanel had also found the will to hold and to overcome. Sensing that Merodach's endless power had, in fact, gone past its peak, just as the limits of his own physical abilities were disturbingly coming into view, now Nethanel gathered himself to make what he knew would be the last attempt to gain a decisive initiative.

During the entire fight, Nethanel had met every thrust on Merodach's part with a steady, equal pressure to ensure that he would not be pushed down the hill behind him. Suddenly, like any champion wrestler would, suddenly, he released his pressure on his opponent's rack. A miniscule gap between the two was created. Within that fraction of a second, Nethanel repositioned his antlers in such a way which, thanks to the tiny space created by the broken brow tine, allowed him to secure a lower, much more stable position with a lot more leverage.

Instantly, Merodach knew that he was done. He had given his all and now he was done. He gave a desperate, futile thrashing of hooves and horns, but now he was appalled to see the final vestiges of his apparently bottomless arrogance give fully away to a mindless panic. He had never been beaten since his youth, so he had absolutely no idea how to retreat in good order. However, when his feet began to slip and his neck started to twist into an unsustainable position, it wasn't long before Merodach felt compelled to rapidly learn the value of discretion. But he was too slow in coming to this conclusion.

Unfortunately for Merodach, Nethanel was not in a forgiving mood. Because of the blind nakedness of the violence, Nethanel was now absolutely intent on administrating the maximum amount of punishment possible. Merodach had gone too far. Nethanel knew that if the tables had been turned that he, Nethanel, would surely receive the same treatment that he was about to mete out.

When his left foot suddenly slipped and rose from the ground, Merodach clumsily and abruptly turned in an attempt to escape. His neck, however, was now so high in the air that Nethanel had no problem smashing his opponent to the ground. As he was bouncing somewhat unceremoniously along, Merodach tried to regain his footing only to be savagely slammed back down on a leaf-strewn ledge by the most powerful thrust of antlers that Nethanel was ever able to muster. The force was so great that one of Nethanel's tines ripped through Merodach's hide and pierced the outer layer of his jugular vein. Emitting a guttural bellow of desperation and horror, Merodach, in an adrenalin laced effort to escape, tore his neck free from the offending tine of Nethanel's rack. In doing so, however, he succeeded in tearing open his jugular vein almost completely.

Running only because of the adrenalin and, initially, with the assistance of Nethanel's pursuing tines, Merodach was able to make it to the very bottom of the gentle slope before his lifeblood began to run out entirely. Taking final shelter under an old, sagging hemlock tree, Merodach lay down and let the cone of his life pass over him. Desperately at first, and then much more calmly, he followed the circle of light showing at the end of the cone until finally the blackness of that cone's walls stretched out, until that light was too far away and too small to pursue any further.

The coydog, Myra, a distant cousin of Athaliah, the mother of Zodac, being an astute hunter and the leader of the dominant pack in her district, had sensed a commotion occurring on the other side of the mountain that she had happened to be near. Moving quickly, she had inadvertently frightened the doe Eloua as that deer was listening intently to something nearby. Myra crested a lower part of the summit just as Merodach released his cry of despair as he tore himself loose from the grasp of Nethanel's rack. In that sound Myra recognized death. Then, through a dense screen of trees, the coydog was able to make out the panicked, somewhat unsteady flight of a defeated buck.

Cautiously, so as not to evoke any further flight, cautiously Myra followed the path of Merodach to his final resting place. The smell of heavy bleeding came up to her from the persistent air currents feeding up the hill, but she gave the deer time to die peacefully. It was well that she continued to use caution as she gingerly approached the ancient hemlock under which Merodach's lifeless body now laid. She got close enough to actually see the big buck's body beneath the tree. However, just as she was about to call out to her distant pack to inform them of the good news, right at that very moment she spotted a curious movement which held that call up in her throat. From just down below her, out of the shadow of some large rocks, a massive, feline form emerged and made its way on up to the fallen Merodach. It was a fully mature, male mountain lion. He had followed a female into a new land and just as he was about to begin feeding, he looked up directly into Myra's eyes and issued a challenge which would define the relationship of their species from that moment on.

It was perhaps fortunate that Merodach had been deposed. Though more than virile enough by any ordinary standard, he had nevertheless been part of a stagnating gene pool which was beginning to go nowhere in an increasingly large, icy brown circle. He represented the white-tail equivalent of a successful dead end. He had been a sturdy building block which, if left in place to support a larger, more complex structure, could have instead ended up contributing to a weakening of his kind. After all, if enough wrong choices are made, then sometimes a species can suffer or even cease to exist altogether.

The reinstatement of a viable mountain lion population into the remote mountains of Maine played well into Nethanel's hand. Already possessed of an active wandering gene, the presence of an expanding lion population tended to promote and exaggerate this wandering tendency in Nethanel's progeny over the short term. If the mountain lion population got too heavy, too insistent, then the descendants of Nethanel were not afraid to move out of what had been their home territory for a long time to find a better place. Though the balance of nature would always ensure that a sudden reversal in a group's good fortune would not precipitate an extinction event in any particular area, that is not to say that some individuals might not take what would ordinarily be considered to be extraordinary steps to not only avoid reversals, but to guarantee rejuvenation and success. And if it wasn't mountain lions, then it would be something else, anything else. When the mood was upon them, they would move quite a ways, sometimes great distances. And, as was also their want, they would always be inclined to make these journeys to the most remote parts of the new territory that they could find.

This tendency persisted through the millenniums. First up into northeast Canada, then back out across Manitoba where Scipio, their most important ancestral contributor, had held court at the northernmost limit of the white-tail world; then onward, westward toward the Pacific until turning southward into Mexico before looping northeast once again. Then, on the way back up through the southeast, then they were temporarily snubbed up by a brief, "limited" nuclear was which brought back a lot of heavy forest land and a decline of white-tail numbers, due to the loss of grasslands.

Every living thing suffered, but the descendants of Nethanel were able to endure, because they had persisted in seeking out the more remote regions of which there were now plenty indeed. With deer numbers drastically reduced, the great cycle around the North American territories began to be speeded up in an effort to build those numbers back up. Eventually, over a huge period of time, eventually a new genetic ice circle appeared, foretelling of stagnation and doom. But the tragic portent of this icy appearance was never realized. That was because, more rapidly than one might imagine, in the wink of a cosmic eye, the sun began to swell and give up its fires, reducing the earth and everything on it to ash and ruin.

However, before all that happened, massive, interstellar arks, guided by the ghosts of human hands, had already departed from mother earth. The arks did not wander aimlessly either. They went to where places had been prepared. There, somewhere just to the right of Antares and all up and down that corridor of the cosmos, on vast planets, new and clean, there they took all manner of creatures, including the white-tail deer. But not just any deer, for the probes had been typically accurate. Not only were these new deer healthy and strong, in order that they might readily mix in with the resident deer populations, not only that, but it was deliberately determined that a certain number of these deer had to possess a strong proclivity for wandering. In this way it was guaranteed that wherever life was strong enough and brave enough, then it, life, would be privileged to witness and appreciate the result of the rise of Nethanel.

FINIS

About the Author

Andrew R. Bennett has lived his entire life in the mountains of western Maine. At a very early age, during the extremely harsh winters of the 1960s, he developed a deep love and respect for the white-tail deer and their ability to survive.

Mr. Bennett graduated in 1976 from the University of Southern Maine with a Bachelor of Science degree. He has written two previous novels, *Playing Bingo,* and *Master Buck.*

www.ingramcontent.com/pod-product-compliance
Lightning Source LLC
Chambersburg PA
CBHW051232130726
47988CB00001B/315